To Jennifer and in memory of
Mum and Dad,
Florence and
Eddie Nicholson-Morton,
my adoptive but true parents.

ROSS MORTON

THE
$300 MAN

Complete and Unabridged

LINFORD
Leicester

First published in Great Britain in 2009 by
Robert Hale Limited
London

First Linford Edition
published 2011
by arrangement with
Robert Hale Limited
London

The moral right of the author has been asserted

British Library CIP Data

Morton, Ross.
The $300 man. - - (Linford western library)
1. Western stories.
2. Large type books.
I. Title II. Series III. Three hundred dollar man
823.9'2–dc22

ISBN 978–1–44480–512–3

Published by
F. A. Thorpe (Publishing)
Anstey, Leicestershire

Set by Words & Graphics Ltd.
Anstey, Leicestershire
Printed and bound in Great Britain by
T. J. International Ltd., Padstow, Cornwall

This book is printed on acid-free paper

THE $300 MAN

What's a life worth? $300, maybe.
Corbin Molina lost a hand during
the Civil War and always carries
$300 — his pay as a substitute
Union soldier. He's on a mission to
Walkerville. When he arrives Corbin
investigates their law and administration and finds that the Walker
family dominates the townspeople
and his questions bring trouble. His
past emerges to confront him during
a tense showdown that threatens not
only him but also his newfound love.

Prologue

The Hook

'Three hundred dollars — that'll do nicely!' said Bert Granger as he finished thumbing through the billfold Corbin Molina had been encouraged to hand over. As added persuasion, Bert held a revolver in his other hand.

Perched on the edge of his aisle seat on the right-hand side of the swaying railway carriage, Corbin was coiled like a spring, biding his time, ready to jump the robbers. The money didn't concern him too much, it was the opened envelope Granger had taken with the cash; if the train-robber read the letter inside he'd more than likely shoot Corbin where he sat. A thin-lipped smile was the only expression on his reddish-brown features as he held his arms aloft, the left one terminating in a stump encased by a metal band and a hook. Further up the carriage was a forest of upheld arms. Corbin's hooded deep brown eyes glared past his hat brim at the train-robber he'd recognized.

'Hey, don't look at me like that, mister.' As Bert spoke he revealed two broken teeth; his voice was high-pitched, as if his unmentionables had been trapped in a vice. 'This may be a lot of greenbacks, but it sure as hell ain't worth dying for!'

'I don't think this is the time or place to discuss the economics of a life,' Corbin said ruefully, his voice husky, 'though I have my own firm opinion on the subject.'

'You talk mighty fine for someone who's just been robbed,' squeaked Bert. He glanced down to read the envelope: 'Molina — what kind of name is that, anyway? Mex, is it?' He screwed up his eyes and rasped a hand over his stubble. 'Yeah, you look half-breed, I reckon.'

Corbin shrugged his broad square

shoulders. He had been called worse; name-calling wasn't worth losing your life over, either.

Bert leaned across and removed Corbin's Frontier Colt revolver, which was riding butt forward on his left hip, and shoved it in his own belt. He eyed Molina's hook but said nothing.

'Can I lower my arms now?'

'Sure, since you're only half a man.' No threat, the rebuke implied.

'Thank you,' said Corbin, shaking his limbs to restore some circulation. He rested his forearms on his thighs, biding his time. Behind him in the aisle was the second bandit, Bert's older brother, Elijah, his dark curly-haired reflection clearly defined in the glass window opposite. Their likenesses had been captured well on the wanted dodgers, along with that of a third brother, Arnie. Maybe Arnie was working another carriage. Elijah, stout and muscular, held a shotgun, randomly threatening one passenger then another with the weapon.

Bert thrust Corbin's money and envelope into a slightly bulging gunny sack hanging from his belt and moved forward. He turned to the middle-aged woman in the seat in front of Corbin, on the left-hand side of the aisle. 'Now, ma'am, what have you got, besides your obvious charms, eh?' He chuckled but she wasn't smiling, her face was pale and her eyes close to tears.

She was modestly dressed in green gingham and wore a white lace bonnet over her mousy hair. 'Please, sir, I have very little,' she pleaded, holding a hand to her chest.

'That ring will do nicely!' Bert growled, grabbing her hand.

'No, please, my late husband gave me — '

'Hey, you cur, leave her be!' An elderly fat man rose to his feet two rows ahead, his Dundreary whiskers bristling, his hands now touching the carriage ceiling. He wore a frock coat and vest with a gold watch chain stretching tautly across his belly.

Wielding his shotgun, Elijah moved forward, next to Corbin, legs braced against the movement of the carriage, and warningly levelled the barrel at the fat man. 'Just wait your turn, mister. I'll have your watch when my brother gets to you!'

Bert laughed and tugged off the woman's wedding band. She whimpered but said nothing.

Elijah chuckled. 'Get another husband, widow. He'll buy a new ring for you!'

These distractions were enough. Half rising, Corbin swung his left arm up, the hook sinking into Elijah's neck. Blood spurted, splashing Corbin's dark-blue flannel shirt and buckskin jacket. Damn, must have hit an artery. Jerking his bloody hook out of the wound, he used it to snag the shotgun out of Elijah's hands.

Bert swerved round, levelling his six-gun, his face draining white at sight of his sibling crumpling to the carriage floor.

Corbin's right hand grabbed the shotgun. Resting the barrel on the back

5

of the seat, he blasted Bert full in the chest before the bandit could fire off a single bullet.

The widow shrieked in alarm as Bert fell back on to the floor, ineffectually gripping his revolver. Others cheered.

Lowering the shotgun to the floor, Corbin knelt down beside Bert and wiped his bloody hook on the man's vest.

'Jeezus,' Bert wheezed, clutching his chest, 'you move fast — '

' . . . for half a man?'

'Aye.' Bert coughed, his gun hand trembling.

Corbin took the revolver off him; there was no strength in the man's hand. 'You won't be needing this where you're going.'

'I guess not. My brother, is he . . . ?'

Corbin nodded. 'Gone to his Maker.' He retrieved his Frontier Colt and shoved it in the holster over his left hip. 'Where's Arnie?'

'You recognized us, eh?'

'Yeah, Bert, you're famous.'

Grinning, Bert coughed up bright red blood. 'We got to be famous, eh?'

'So you did — dead famous. Now where's Arnie?'

Bert grimaced. 'I ain't saying.' He trembled and the fear of death animated his eyes. 'He ain't going to be best pleased, Elijah and me dying, an' all.'

'You should've taken up an honest profession, then,' Corbin said unsympathetically, rummaging in the gunny sack. He withdrew his envelope and the wad of bank notes. 'You were right,' he added, 'this money ain't worth dying for.'

Bert nodded, unable to speak, and his broken-toothed grin froze as the light went out of his eyes.

Pocketing his money and envelope in his buckskin jacket, Corbin ignored the shouts and cheers of the relieved passengers. He stood up and passed the sack to the rear of the carriage so the contents could be restored to the rightful owners.

Corbin bowed to the distraught

woman and handed her the wedding band. 'Yours, ma'am.'

Her hazel eyes widened as she noticed his bloodstained shirt and jacket. She swallowed, nodded and snatched the ring and put it on a trembling finger. He'd seen similar reactions before. People of a delicate sensibility tended to feel uncomfortable near him when violence erupted.

He was his own worst enemy, he opined. He wanted anonymity, but this sure wasn't the way to go about it.

'You're a hero, sir!' exclaimed the fat man, tapping him on the shoulder. As Corbin turned, the man added, 'If you're ever looking for work, don't hesitate to look me up — here's my card!'

Corbin scanned it: *Oliver Magruder, Oil and Tar Specialist*. He smiled and fingered the brim of his black slouch hat. 'Thanks, Mr Magruder. I hope you don't mind me saying, but that was foolhardy of you to voice your objections, though you sure gave me the chance to take them on.'

Blood drained from Magruder's face. 'You think they'd have shot me?'

'Some might have.'

'I never gave it a thought. I was just so incensed, the way they treated this poor lady.'

'Gallant of you, sir, but I'd advise you to be careful in future. Some bandits shoot first and argue afterwards.'

Magruder sighed and shook his head. 'Knowing all this, you still — as you say — took them on?'

'I've a little experience in dishing out violence, sir. It comes in handy,' Corbin said, smiling lopsidedly as he gestured with his hook.

'Well, you're still a hero in my book, Mr Molina.'

'Really, I don't want any fuss.' He turned away from Magruder. Pointing to two heavy-set men further up the aisle, he said, 'You can help me move these corpses to the rear of the carriage, where they'll cause the least distress till we get to Retribution.'

Both men were only too willing to help.

The widow fanned herself and tried to concentrate on the passing barren country. Her eyes widened for a second as their carriage passed a man mounted on a piebald at the edge of the permanent way's embankment. He was holding the reins of two other horses and there was a look of puzzlement on his face, as if he'd been expecting the train to stop for him.

1

Heaven's Gateway

Banners strung across the main street announced that in a week's time Retribution would be celebrating its twentieth year since its founding day way back on 19 July, 1853. Corbin wasn't in any mood for rejoicing: he'd killed two men.

The train's stop hadn't been scheduled for much longer than forty minutes, enough time for passengers to get on or off and for water to be transferred to the engine. But the two bodies had to be removed and accounted for, and that took time, especially with Sheriff Ralph Deshler going by the book. If he hadn't intended staying overnight in town Corbin would have sneaked away without bothering with the lawman. The reward money was of no consequence. As it was, the sheriff had asked him to fill in a statement.

Corbin promised to join the sheriff, but first needed to change his blood-stained clothes. He held up a fresh shirt and jacket which he'd taken out of his bag, folded them and put them in his valise. 'Is there a laundry I could use?'

'Sure, Ma Chong's — behind my office, as a matter of fact.'

'Fine. Let's go, then, Sheriff,' he said, and stepped alongside the lawman.

Deshler was in his forties. Business-like, tall and lean, he wore a narrow moustache and denim jacket and jeans. Gesturing with his battered wide-brimmed Stetson, he sent his two deputies off to organize the removal of the bodies. Corbin liked the man; he was affable and seemed quite relieved. As he said, cleaning up after a death was preferable to having to face death itself.

'How long you staying in Retribution, Mr Molina?' Deshler asked as they strolled down the street. Corbin declined the offer of a Bull Durham roll-up.

'Just tonight.' He hefted a small valise with his hook. 'This is just an overnight bag. I sent my luggage on to the depot — I'll be catching the stage for Walkerville in the morning.'

Deshler scratched a sulphur match and lit up. 'Good — it leaves nine sharp. Be on it.'

Corbin eyed the sheriff and raised an eyebrow. 'What does that mean?'

'Once their brother gets to hear about this, Arnie Granger will be gunning for you, I warrant. I'd rather he found you somewhere else, not in Retribution. Besides, our undertaker has enough to do, thanks.'

'Granger will only come looking for me if someone tells him.'

The sheriff blew smoke and thumbed his chest. 'I won't be saying a word. But someone's bound to gab, you can be sure of that.'

True enough, Corbin mused. Information was worth a few dollars to the right ear.

13

They stepped up on to the boardwalk and the sheriff unlocked his office door. 'Come in, let's settle accounts.'

'I didn't do it for the money, Sheriff. I'm no bounty hunter.'

'Hell, I know that. But you risked your life so you might as well get paid for it. Let's be honest, it ain't my money.'

Corbin nodded, conceiving that he might be able to put the reward money, whatever it amounted to, to good use.

Sheriff Deshler unlocked the big cast-iron safe behind his desk and counted out $400. 'That's two for each villain. Another two, if you get Arnie.'

Folding the money in his jacket, Corbin shook his head. 'It seems like blood money, Sheriff.'

'No, it doesn't, son. It's what it says on the dodgers, a reward, that's all. And I reckon it's worth every penny if it means folk can sleep better at night knowing those varmints ain't going to trouble no one.' He slid a thin ledger across. 'Sign here, please.'

Corbin picked up a pen, dabbed the nib in the inkpot on the desk and scrawled his name with a flourish. Then he straightened up and he flipped his hat back off his brow. 'Now can you tell me where Mae Begley's establishment is, please?'

Deshler chuckled. 'You must be wanting Heaven's Gateway, as she calls it. So, you intend spending the reward money there, eh?'

'Possibly.'

'It's three blocks short of the other end of town. Used to be on the outskirts, since so-called decent folk didn't want anything to do with her place, but now it's sort of in the middle since the town's grown over the years.'

'Thanks, Sheriff.' Shaking Deshler's hand, Corbin said, 'See you around.'

'Aye, maybe you will. Steer clear of squint-eyed Susan; she's a mite too fiery for anyone's taste, if you ask me.'

'Oh, the woman I've come to see isn't called Susan,' Corbin said and strode out through the door.

Heaven's Gateway was an imposing edifice, its three storeys dwarfing the neighbouring shops and offices. Its entrance portico boasted granite pillars and steps, while the boardwalk that ran round the building was of varnished teak. Drapes of a variety of red hues adorned the windows; balustraded balconies on the two upper floors were colourfully festooned with women wearing long silk dresses and low necklines.

Having changed his clothes in the back of Ma Chong's, Corbin felt slightly better as he approached the bordello. A ginger-haired soiled dove leaned over the rail, a black cigarita in her hand. She called out, 'Hey, mister, ask for Ginger — I can give you a good time — all night for thirty dollars.'

He paused and removed his black slouch hat. 'Thanks kindly, ma'am, but I've a prior booking.' He climbed the steps and, standing in the shade of the balcony, he pulled the bell.

He heard Ginger swear. 'Since when did Ma Begley take bookings?'

The door was opened by a woman in a striking bright red dress. He was no expert, but she appeared to be in her forties. Her cheeks harboured too much rouge. Her red hair clashed with the colour of her dress; it was pulled back in a chignon decorated with a thin green bandanna; large silver earrings dangled. Her blue-green eyes appraised him in the flick of two black-painted eyelids. Doubtless gauging his profitability, he opined. She let her gaze linger a second or two on his hook, then smiled.

'So, you'll be wanting a girl, I take it?' she declared in a thick Irish brogue.

Stating the obvious, he felt like responding. Instead, he said, 'Yes.' It would be easier this way, he reckoned.

'Well, come in.' She stood aside, swept the slight train of her dress behind her and gestured for him to enter the hallway. She shut the door and said, 'You've come to the right place, to be sure. Hang your hat, mister.'

He hung the slouch on a mahogany hook by the door.

Turning on her heel with a swishing sound of satin, she said, 'Follow me, sir.'

He did so, trailing behind her swaying red bustle as it swept over the narrow strip of hall carpet. Even though it was still day, wall sconces were lit, projecting a warm ruddy glow everywhere Corbin looked. There was a sickly-sweet smell of cheap perfume which, he surmised, probably served to keep at bay the pungent aroma of body odour and tobacco smoke. He heard murmuring up ahead.

Once he had passed through an arched doorway, a heavy brocade curtain fell behind him and all sound ceased. They were in a large room, each wall lined with two or three *chaiselongues*, the walls papered in a crimson flock design. Seats were either occupied by young women with painted faces or anxious-looking men of all ages. The women wore white dimity wide skirts and soft ringlets of hair cascaded over bare shoulders; some fluttered lace fans in front of dark coquettish eyes. Most of the men only gave him a cursory look then returned to studying their boots or chatting to each other; the women too resumed their conversation, ignoring him. It was as if they were all congregated in a railway station waiting room. Only here the tickets were to Paradise, even if it was ephemeral.

At the far end of the room was a wide staircase which was carpeted in red and curved up to the second floor with its balconies and doors; doubtless a similar staircase climbed to the third floor.

'We're a mite busy at the moment,' explained Madam Begley, gently nudging his arm. 'Always the same when a train comes in.' She glanced up at him, her hands clasped demurely in front. 'Do you have any preferences?'

'Pardon?'

'Blonde, brunette, black — hair, that

19

is. We have all kinds of skin shades as well. Do you like your women lissom or generous?'

'I'd like to pay for time with just one of your girls, ma'am,' he said. 'Her name's Jean — Jean Pegram.'

'Jeannie?' Her features clouded and she shrugged. 'You'd better come back tomorrow, then. She's got an all-nighter — '

The low murmurs of the room were suddenly disturbed by a high-pitched scream. Madam Begley's face suffused purple and her eyes narrowed. 'That's her, poor bitch!' She lifted her skirts to ascend the stairs. 'That swine, he promised!'

Swiftly brushing past the madam, Corbin loped up the stairs two at a time. At the top, he hesitated, but the scream came again, chilling his blood — from his right. He pounded along the carpeted floor and entered a passageway. On each side were doors bearing nameplates. He was sure that the sound had come from further down

20

and he passed Angelique, Maud, Pauline, Rebecca, and Susan — squint-eyed Susan? As he paused at the door marked Jeannie, he felt his heart hammering with old emotions.

He reached for the door handle but a heavy grating voice came from inside the room and he froze, listening. 'I paid for all night. That means I can do what the hell I like with you!'

'No, Mr Turner, you've been told — not the knife!'

Corbin's jaw tightened and his eyes narrowed. He now tried the handle. It wasn't locked and he swung the door wide; it bashed noisily against some furniture and porcelain rattled. He drew his Colt.

Jeannie's bare back was to him as she knelt at the foot of the bed, her long copper-coloured hair hanging loose. The rumpled sheets were splattered with droplets of blood. Brandishing a knife, its blade dripping, a grey-bearded man in red long johns leaned on the brass bedpost. Jeannie was so intent on the knife, she didn't respond to Corbin's intrusion. The man, Turner, snarled and swore, seeing Corbin in the doorway.

Cocking his Colt, Corbin said, 'Don't make another move, Turner, or it'll be your last!'

'Who in tarnation are you? You've got no right to interfere!'

'I have every right, since I have the gun. Now, drop that blade. Slowly.'

The knife clattered to the bare boards. Jeannie glanced briefly over her shoulder, her hazel eyes streaked with tears, and hugged a sheet to her; small patches of blood soaked into the linen.

Corbin's heart did a small flip of recognition. Ignoring the sight of Jeannie's blood and her sobbing, he said, 'Sensible man.' He gestured with his six-gun. 'Now, come with me. You have an appointment with Sheriff Deshler.'

Turner hesitated, glancing back at the chair in the corner. 'My trousers, I need — '

'You need to be quiet.' Corbin noted the pleading in the man's eyes but shook his head. 'You go as you are — or you go feet first. Your choice.'

Scowling, Turner walked past the trembling form of Jeannie, edged by Corbin and stepped out into the passage.

Madam Begley was standing there, her arms akimbo. Behind her clustered four girls and two men. 'Bejesus, Mr Turner, you've been warned about that dad-blamed knife before!' Mrs Begley wagged a ring-laden finger at the man. 'This will not do! You're barred from stepping foot in my house ever again!'

'You mean he's done this before?' Corbin asked, jabbing the barrel of his revolver into the small of Turner's back.

'Unfortunately, yes. But he's an important man in the town. We have to make allowances.'

Brusquely brushing past her, Corbin shoved Turner ahead of him. He growled over his shoulder, 'Make sure Jeannie is doctored and cleaned up when I return, madam!'

* ★ ★

He rapped on the door with his hook.

'Who is it?' Jeannie's voice was throaty and tremulous; perhaps a little rougher round the edges than he remembered.

'It's the man who saved you from Turner's knife.'

'Yes, of course, Mrs Begley said you'd be back.'

The key in the lock turned.

He thought it odd that she should lock the door now, though not while she was being intimate with her customers.

He heard her move away from the door and some wooden furniture creaked. 'Come in,' she said.

Opening the door, he tried to smother the memory from an hour earlier, when Jeannie had been threatened and bleeding. He entered the room, taking off his hat, and closed the door after him.

She sat in a rocking-chair. Looking at him from hollowed eye-sockets, she seemed malnourished. The jutting cones of her breasts were more pronounced than he recalled, pressing against some white gauzy material, while her legs were covered by a white frilly petticoat. Her feet were bare. She hadn't managed to clean away all the blood, he noticed; there were traces on the bridge of her left foot.

'Thank you for stopping Mr Turner, sir,' she said, and offered a lopsided smile.

Her smile hadn't been that way before, he realized. Something had altered her face — her nose still turned up at the tip, but it had been broken and was now slightly askew. The freckles were barely noticeable under the powder. Her thin lips usually offered the promise of a winsome smile but now they were dark red and unnatural. At one time her hazel eyes sent his heart soaring when she looked at him, but now she was hardly focusing on him or her world. Her mind was in some dark and distant place. Life once brimmed from her, now it was little more than a flickering candle in a gale.

'Have your cuts been doctored?'

She blinked, returning from her reverie, and nodded. 'Mrs Begley brought in Doc Bassett. He sewed up two cuts and the rest weren't too deep. The iodine stings, but he says I'll be OK.'

'Just keep the wounds clean,' Corbin said. He refrained from commenting on how many young lives he'd witnessed being snuffed out on account of dirty wounds.

'Thank you for caring, mister.' Her smile was thin, fragile, as if she was afraid that it might be misconstrued, his kindness sullied.

Hands gripping the brim of his hat, he said, 'You don't recognize me, Jean, do you?'

'No, I can't say as I do.' She gave him another travesty of a smile. 'You appreciate, I entertain many gentlemen. Unfortunately, my memory isn't as good as it was, you know?' She lowered her feet to the floorboards and thrust herself out of the chair, which creaked in protest at being abandoned.

'Let me take a good look at you,' she said, gliding up to him. She still walked with an enchanting serene movement; once, he'd thought of her as poetry in motion.

He looked down at her and he could see the stirrings of memory reasserting something in her, in the glinting of her eyes.

Brow wrinkled, she glanced at his hook and then his skewed nose. 'We make a good pair, don't we?' she said.

'Yes, I guess we do.'

She eyed the small scar on his forehead. Reaching up, she brushed a hand gently through his black hair, lingering on the clump of white hair on the left, just above the scar. At one time her touch would have sent his heart pounding; now he just felt sad. At last, her gaze lingered on his. There was no mistake. Recognition widened her eyes and moisture formed at the rims. She stepped back a pace, a hand rising to her chest, over her heart. What little colour she had seemed to drain from her face. 'Corbin? Is it really you?'

'Yes.'

'Oh, my God,' she whispered, turning away. She crossed over to the bed and sat down, studying her feet and let tears fall to the floor where they darkened the dust and wood. 'Oh, my God.' A small fist beat at her right breast, pitifully.

He moved to sit beside her on the bed but refrained from touching her. 'It's been a long time, Jean.'

She nodded. 'A lifetime.'

Having observed the change wrought in her, he could understand how she must feel. He'd last seen her in '62 — twelve years ago.

'You've changed,' she said, her hands resting in her lap. Turning her head, she studied him, her eyes ranging over his broad shoulders and muscular arms and thighs. 'You're taller, bigger — quite a man now, Corbin.' She shook her head.

'I didn't know about the hand — well, anything really.'

He could feel the trembling of her body transmitted through the bed's mattress. At any other time he might have appreciated the irony of sitting here on a bed with her; in those far-off days he had coveted her young nubile form, though he hadn't rightly understood all the emotions that had threshed through his adolescent frame. Now, he understood all too well.

Gently, he placed his hand on hers. 'Life changes us, Jean. I've been through a war — and a lot besides.'

She gave a wan smile. 'You don't want to know what I've endured, Corbin. You really don't.' She looked away again, the back of her hand wiping the tears from mottled cheeks. 'Best you just go and leave me be.'

Corbin shook his head. 'No, Jean, I came to see you. I'm not leaving.'

She faced him again, her eyes wide with a cynical edge to them, which he found surprisingly distasteful. Her upper lip curled. 'You want me, is that it?'

'No, Jean. I didn't turn up here as a customer.'

'Client,' she corrected.

'Whatever. As it happens, you're the fourth Jean I've tracked down. The others were false trails.'

'Tracked down?'

'Oh, I haven't made it my business. Sometimes, though, in my travels, I get to hear about a woman called Jean and the description seems to fit yours.' He eyed her copper-coloured hair and felt impelled to stroke it, as if that motion would brush away the past so they could return to those times of innocence. He raised a hand and gestured vaguely. 'So I take a detour, just to put my mind at rest. Today, my detour found the real Jean.'

'But why are you looking for me?' Her eyes shone with a forlorn hope.

'I wanted to be sure that you're all right. And there are a few things I need to know — things only you can tell me.'

★ ★ ★

Strange, how some memories had sustained him through the fighting. Then, afterwards, when he learned the truth, he tried so hard to deny those selfsame memories. Yet, despite the heartache, they were his past, part of the fabric that made him what he was, who he was.

Twelve years ago. It had been a glorious hot September day and his heart was racing with conflicting emotions as he sat beside willowy Jean Pegram on the riverbank. 'I know I'll be going away,' he had said, 'but when it's all over — they say it won't last much longer — I'll have three hundred dollars to set us up in a place of our own.'

'Where'd you get that kind of money, Corbin?'

'It's the bounty they pay for volunteers,' he lied. This had been the excuse he'd concocted, which wasn't too far from the truth, save that the federal bounty only amounted to $100. 'It's good, honest money.'

'But you might be killed! No amount of money is worth your life.'

He grinned. When you're young, you feel immortal. 'The Rebs can't sustain their defiance. The Union will trample all over them soon enough!'

Jean wrung her long slender hands. 'That's silly talk by politicians, and you know it! Haven't you been reading the papers?'

'Papers go hang!' he snapped, his face twisting in frustration. 'I'm doing this for you, Jean!' He gripped her hands. 'Will you wait for me?'

Tears glistened in her hazel eyes. She didn't seem capable of speech so she simply nodded.

Corbin sighed and let go. 'That's settled then. Your love will support me through the trials to come,' he promised.

'That sounds like one of your silly poetry books!' Jean said and burst into tears. Then, ignoring his fumbling outstretched arms, she struggled to her feet and ran towards her home.

Girls, he thought. So emotional. Must make allowances, though, since she was only fifteen. He was a year older and more mature. Mature enough to falsify his age.

Of course he never explained to Jean why he was joining the army. When the State had fallen short of its quota of volunteers, the authorities were obliged to apply the draft, calling up all able-bodied men between the ages of eighteen and forty-five until the numbers required were met.

'Corby, I've been drafted into the army,' Sam Buford had said that August morning when storm clouds hovered over the ranch. He smoothed out the crumpled sheet of paper and showed it to Corbin.

The pair of them sat on the wide windowsill, watching as the cloudburst shut visibility outside to a mere few feet. 'I can't leave Pa to work the ranch alone,' Sam had moaned, brushing a hand through his thick sandy hair.

'Heck, I don't know what to do!'

Corbin's heart went out to his best friend. After all, Jubal Buford had taken Corbin in when he was a young orphan. Sure, Mr Buford used the punishing belt on him, often when the transgression was Sam's in fact, but he always knew that the old man never meant to hurt him even though he invariably said something like, 'I'm gonna whale the tar outta ya!' Mr Buford was obliged to inflict punishment to appease his wife. Despite that belt, he loved the old man like his father. 'If I could go instead, Sam, I would.'

Abruptly, Sam jumped down off the sill and gripped Corbin's arm. 'D'you mean that, Corby?'

Corbin shrugged. 'Sure.'

Fists resting on slim hips, Sam exclaimed, 'If I paid you three hundred dollars, you could take my place!'

'Three hundred dollars?'

'Yes, it's allowed, see. You go in my place, as my substitute, and it's all legal, because I'll have paid you.'

'Go soldiering, me?' Corbin laughed. 'It might be an adventure, at that.' Then he paused, thoughtful. 'But what about Jean? I'd have to leave her. She might not wait for me, Sam.' He let out a sigh. 'The thought of losing her, it makes me think maybe I shouldn't go — '

'Think, Corby!' Sam's greyish-brown eyes were alight with the idea. 'You'll have three hundred dollars to buy a place of your own, somewhere you and Jean can share!'

Corbin grinned. 'Yes, that's true. And I'll get regular pay, as well. Heck, I could be a millionaire in no time!'

'So, you'll do it for me?'

Corbin nodded. 'Yes, I will. What have I got to do, exactly?'

Sam winked and patted a finger against his pug nose. 'Leave it to me.'

Sam arranged everything, especially the paperwork concerning the substitution and adding two years to Corbin's certificate of birth. Sam also insisted on not telling his father. 'It's best if you just sneak off one night, Corby, otherwise Pa is likely to object, knowing your birthdate and all.'

Although it pained him to run off in the night, Corbin saw the sense in it. After all, it was to help Mr Buford that he was going to war. To repay him for his kindnesses, too.

Sam and Corbin had embraced in the barn and then parted. Twelve years ago, in 1862. 'Oh, my God, what a fool I was!' Jean lamented now as they sat fully clothed, their backs against the bedhead, sharing a bottle of whiskey.

'You and me too,' Corbin agreed. Thoughtful, he sipped from his tumbler. 'Tell me.'

The liquor had loosened Jean's tongue. 'Mr Buford never cottoned on why you up and left without any explanation,' she began. Being a neighbour's daughter and too young besides, Jean felt unable to tell the old man that Corbin had joined the army. It seemed to Jean that Mr Buford simply wasted away with grief over the next six months. Buford's wife didn't help, either. She'd always made life awkward for Corbin, despite his good friendship with her son, Sam. More than once, Mrs Buford had snapped at her husband, 'Blood will out. I told you he was a no-good mestizo!'

Jean had wept into her pillow for many weeks after Corbin ran off to join the army. Then one morning she decided that she would not fret for him or wait any longer. It was unconscionable of him to expect it of her. She was becoming a young woman and couldn't waste away while not knowing if Corbin lived or died.

The truth was that she was mighty pleased to learn that Sam was showing strong interest in her.

That starry night behind the barn, when Sam promised to marry her, she gave in to his fumbling overtures. Their coupling hadn't been as she'd dreamed from those sensational stories she read. Yet, surprisingly, the more they did it, the more she wanted it. Trouble was, he never did marry her.

'When Mr Buford died, his widow sold up and we all moved — where the pickings were rich, Mrs Buford said.'

Corbin took a drink from his tumbler. 'You went with Sam?'

'Yes, he was still stringing me along. Said we'd get married once we'd settled.'

'Until you came to Retribution?'

She tipped the tumbler of whiskey to her mouth and swallowed; she pulled a face but Corbin thought that it had nothing to do with the liquor's strength or taste. 'Yes. I don't know what happened, Corbin. I passed out one night and the next thing I knew I was here.' Her voice croaked and her eyes momentarily darkened at the memory. 'In the basement.'

Jean had been surprised to find that she wasn't alone down there. Two other young women were held captive; Monica and Lisa. Naturally, Jean had thought of trying to escape — until she saw what happened to Monica. Mrs Begley's brothers Mort and Rufus used a stick on the soles of the poor girl's feet; Monica was hobbling for weeks after she received that cruel punishment. 'We don't aim to stop you working, honey,' the madam told her. 'You can still lie down and earn, but you sure as hell won't be able to run away!'

Mort and Rufus Begley enjoyed obliging their big sister. 'Break them in for me, boys,' she told them. 'I want them pliant and docile, just like the clients want.'

Gradually, over time, Jean learned the trade of a crib girl, mislaid her self-respect in the process and stayed; in truth, she had no other trade, nowhere to go and little money. 'I have food and board and Mrs Begley pays us each month.' By now it was late and her eyelids were drooping. 'Not much money, I know, since some goes to pay off my indenture. But I can save up to buy nice things from the general store or the catalogue.'

Gritting his teeth, Corbin gazed

around the small room. The drapes were threadbare and dusty; the patch of carpet at the foot of the bed was worn and stained. At least the bedclothes were clean. A narrow closet stood against the far wall, its door hanging open on a faulty hinge; inside he glimpsed four dresses and two pairs of shoes on the closet's floor. A chipped porcelain washbasin and water jug stood on top of a tallboy.

'Are Mort and Rufus still here?' he asked, his voice husky.

She hunkered down in the bed and drowsily shook her head. 'No, they skedaddled at about the same time as the bank was robbed.' She laughed hollowly, nursing her empty glass. 'Mrs Begley wasn't best pleased, I can tell you!' Smiling at the memory, she fell asleep.

Gently moving off the bed, Corbin took the tumbler out of her hand and pulled the covers over her.

He padded over to the window and pulled the curtain open. Come daylight, he'd wake up, in time for the Walkerville stage. He sat in the rocking chair and rested his Colt in his lap. He earnestly hoped that Walkerville wasn't going to be as bad as Neboville and Ashkelon.

Consigning those memories to the back of his mind, he lowered his lids and dozed.

2

Worth Living

While Corbin Molina slept, his destination Walkerville — almost two days away by stagecoach — was slumbering too. Except for Grace and Sidney Tuttle, who were rudely awoken by insistent banging on their back door.

Mumbling into his bristling russet beard, Sidney swung his thick sturdy legs out of bed and shoved his broad feet into slippers.

'Who could want you at this time of night?' Grace said, pulling the covers up to her pointed chin.

'It must be important, honey, to be calling this late.' He lit the lantern on the nightstand by his side of the bed and its buttery glow illuminated their second storey bedroom; their drab-coloured clothes hung in one corner, while a heavy oak chest of drawers ran along the wall at the foot of the brass and iron bedstead.

Shuffling to the rear window, Sidney slid it up and hollered, 'Hold your horses, I'll be right down!'

'Hurry up, Tuttle, damn you! We haven't got all night!'

We? Shutting the window, Sidney cast a glance at his wife.

Grace gasped, her hazel eyes wide. 'Don't go, Sid. Sounds like that Rufus Begley fellow. He's up to no good!'

Shrugging his overcoat on top of his long johns, Sidney growled, 'He's big enough to knock the door in, honey. I'd better see what he wants. Probably out of tobacco.' Carrying the lantern, he opened the door and padded over the floor-boards of the landing and down the stairs. Once at the bottom, he edged past the counter and went through the door to the kitchen at the rear. This was directly under their bedroom.

'Come on, Tuttle!' A fist pounded again on the back door.

Sidney unbolted top and bottom and turned the key in the lock. No sooner had he done so than the door swung wide, almost knocking him over. He stepped back a pace.

'Rufus, why the rush? Is there a fire or something?'

Tall and muscular, with a bullet-head, Rufus Begley growled, 'I need shells, plenty of them.' Saddlebags were slung over his left shoulder, suggesting he was about to ride out of town.

Sidney feared the man might have robbed the bank, but it didn't seem likely, the saddlebags weren't exactly bulging with loot. 'Now?'

'Yes, damn you, now!'

'What, have the Indians come back?'

'Stop asking so many tomfool questions and serve your customer!'

Docilely nodding, Sidney shut the back door and locked it. 'Follow me into the shop,' he said and shuffled past Rufus.

The boxes of cartridges were behind the counter. 'Calibre?' he asked in his best business voice.

'Gimme .44s — for Winchesters.'

More than one rifle, then, Sidney thought. He pulled out six boxes from the shelf and put them on the counter.

'At least ten boxes, Tuttle, and be quick about it!'

'Right.' His fingers fumbling, he stacked the required number of boxes. 'That'll be — '

'Put it on Mr Walker's account,' Rufus said, stuffing the boxes into his saddlebags. He turned on his heel and strode, his gait bowlegged, towards the back door. 'If anyone asks, I wasn't here tonight,' he flung over his shoulder as he unlocked the door, opened it and stepped out into the darkness.

Using a sleeve to wipe away the sweat from his forehead, Sidney rushed to the door and locked and bolted it again. He should go out and rouse Sheriff Clegg, but he knew it wouldn't do much good. The man's heart was in the right place, but the lawman's sense of survival seemed to override certain issues.

'On Mr Walker's account, my eye!'

45

Grace said from the foot of the stairs.

Indeed, Sidney thought. 'Let's just go back to bed, honey,' he said, taking her arm.

She shrugged his hand off and stepped up a tread so she could be face to face with him. 'Walker and his cronies are bleeding us dry, Sid. We can't go on like this much longer!'

'I don't have a choice, honey. This has been Walker's town for nigh on eight years.'

'You used to fight for your beliefs, for your family, Sidney Tuttle.'

He exhaled noisily. 'I was young, then. Now, I don't want any trouble; all I want is peace and quiet.'

She laughed without humour. 'You'll soon get your wish, Sid. When you're in Boot Hill, you'll get all the peace and quiet you'll ever need.'

'Maybe, but I don't want to hasten that day by standing up to Mr Walker.'

'And his gunmen,' she added, her tone conceding the unpalatable common sense of his stance.

★ ★ ★

Smoke spiralled up from the Winchesters of the six gunmen who surrounded the homestead. The night was filled with the after-echo from several hundred rounds of ammunition being fired. It was dark but out here the starlight and the moon's glow provided sufficient visibility, though Mort reckoned the shadows were threatening. Since he was a kid, he'd feared shadows. Maybe because his pa came at him so often out of that darkness. He wiped the sweat of memories away and leaned forward in his saddle, hands on the pommel. He tasted the gun smoke and spat on the ground. He could see the roofed portico, its pillars pitted with bullet holes; the two wooden chairs and the small three-legged table barely resembled their original shape, so many shells had peppered into them. The bullet-riddled front door was slightly ajar and a white flag was wafting up and down on the end of a Henry repeater rifle.

'That was just a playful warning, Mr Pike,' Mort called, his saddle leather creaking. 'Are you going to move out peaceable like?'

'Yes, just don't harm my family!'

'You've got a deal, mister!' Mort eased in the saddle, turned to Angus McLaughlin and nodded.

McLaughlin gestured 'OK' with a hand and backed his roan out of sight.

Mort heard McLaughlin giving his three men orders, then they rode quietly towards the hills.

Following a signal from Mort, Reed drove two horses which pulled a small wagon to the front of the building, where he halted the team and engaged the brake. 'The wagon's waiting!' Reed bawled.

'I'm coming out, don't shoot!' Pike called.

Reed tied the reins round the brake handle and jumped down on to the hard-packed earth. He stood back, arms akimbo, and watched.

Pike came out, his long face pale in

the lamplight, eyes staring. His slight frame struggled under the weight of a grandfather clock. Carefully, he put it down in the back of the wagon. About a minute later he was followed by his wife, a straw blonde with a stout frame. She carried a box that chinked a lot as she moved: the family china, Mort guessed. A boy aged about ten stepped out, a box of books in his arms. The entire family were dressed in their Sunday best. After the second trip with prized possessions, Reed strode over to Pike and they had a heated conversation. Eventually Pike nodded and continued to load the wagon. The Pikes returned three more times, piling into the back of the wagon food rations, clothes and a few heirlooms.

'Are you done yet?' Mort shouted, exasperation in his voice.

Pike waved hastily. 'Yes, I'm just securing the load!' As he slung rope over their worldly goods, tethering it on cleats, his wife and son settled themselves on the wagon seat. A few minutes later Pike climbed up, took the reins and let off the brake.

Mort fired a single rifle shot into the air.

The horses whickered.

'Hold it right there!' Mort barked.

Pike glared, his eyes narrowed. 'You promised we could leave unharmed!' he blustered.

'Sure — if you leave the deeds of your property, as *you* promised!'

Shakily, Pike pointed at the open door. 'They're on the table — all the documents, honest!'

'Reed, go check!' Mort ordered.

Nonchalantly loping round the wagon, Reed stepped up on to the boards and ducked his head to enter the doorway. A few anxious seconds later, he emerged, waving the papers in his left hand. 'All here!'

Mort nodded. 'OK, Mr Pike, you can go now.'

'Th-thank you.' Pike geed up the horses. They bucked and jolted along the road, towards the hills, away from their home. Not one of them looked back.

Mort nudged upwards the brim of his hat and scratched his forehead. 'Nice doing business with you, Mr Pike.'

* * *

With a heavy heart, Linus Pike steered the wagon over the rutted road, glancing fearfully over his shoulder. The darkness played tricks, he knew that, but he was sure that he'd heard the snickering of horses behind them. He was reluctant to tell Martha or Jimmy. It was bad enough that they'd been forced out of their home and off their land.

'I still say we should go into town, Linus,' Martha said, hugging her patchwork shawl round her shoulders. 'Sheriff Clegg should be told what has happened.'

'Can't go there, Martha. That Reed fellow said I had to head into the mountains. If we were to go into town, they'd . . . well, he was quite plain what they'd do!'

Martha peered into the back of the wagon and she heaved a motherly sigh at sight of her son under the grey-and-blue blanket. 'Thank the Lord, he's asleep, poor mite.'

'I'm sorry, dear. We've lost everything.'

She grasped his arm and gave him a hug. 'Not everything, Linus. I rescued all our savings and they're inside the teapot! And I'm wearing all my jewellery.' She held up a hand with the diamond ring on it, a treasured heirloom.

He grinned and urged the horses on. He sensed a slight easing of the weight on his shoulders. His heart went out to his wife because she must know that her precious jewellery would have to be sold unless their luck changed.

From time to time he still glanced back, but there was no sign of anyone following.

Soon, they would stop and camp for the night. He'd make sure the Henry was loaded and ready. Daybreak seemed a long way off.

*   *   *

It was late, but some townspeople were still awake; particularly those whose honesty was questionable. The man-servant's eyes seemed sleep deprived, with purple bags under them. Dutifully, he showed Mort into the library and announced him with a distinct tone of opprobrium that was completely lost on Begley.

Mr Walker sat at his desk, his head of thinning salt-and-pepper hair lowered. Walker was stout and barrel-chested with square shoulders. 'You may retire, Wain,' he said gruffly.

'Very good, sir.' Without moving a contour of his face, Wain bowed and left, shutting the door behind him.

Mort waited, hat clasped in his big hands.

After a few long minutes Walker finished writing in the pages of a ledger, lowered his pen and leaned back to show off his middle-age spread. 'You have something for me?' His voice came out as a hoarse whisper.

Nervously running a hand through his curly red hair, Mort nodded. 'Yes, sir.' He delved inside his vest and held out the deeds for the Pike homestead. 'All the papers you wanted.'

Walker snatched them, opened up the documents and avidly scanned the pages. He made a guttural sound in his throat and looked up, hawk-brown eyes piercing Mort. 'You've done well.'

'Thank you, sir.'

Opening the left-hand drawer, Walker lifted out a slightly bulging leather pouch. He weighed it in his palm. 'Your payment,' he said, tossing it to Mort.

'Thanks, sir.'

'What about the Pikes?'

'Well on their way to their final destination, sir.'

'Glad to hear it.' He wafted the

documents at Mort. 'You may go. Spend the money wisely.'

'Right. Yes. I'll do that, Mr Walker.' He closed the door quietly after him.

Walker opened the bottom drawer and slid the documents in. 'One more piece.' He closed and locked the drawer, then stood up. He crossed over to the drinks cabinet and poured two fingers of bourbon. Savouring the liquor, he knew that he would sleep well tonight.

* * *

Sunlight streamed through the grimy window; it was already warm and the creaking wood of the building promised that it was going to be a hot day. Not ideal for a stagecoach journey. Bare to the waist, Corbin poured some water from the jug into the china basin. He soaked his neckerchief then used it one-handed to wipe his face, pleased with the relative coolness; his bristles rasped slightly: a shave could wait till he got to his hotel room in Walkerville. Wrapping one end of the cloth round his hook, he wrung it tightly, then expertly twirled it and whipped the bandanna round his neck, tying a knot with slick fingers and thumb.

'I see you're coping with just the one hand,' mumbled Jean from the bedcovers.

He caught his reflection in the dressing-table mirror. The metal band was connected to a combination of leather and metal, a brace structure that ran up his left arm, across his back and around both shoulders. Most evenings he'd remove it, but not last night. 'I've got used to it,' he said, turning. This morning he'd clipped on the double hook and now used this to snag the shirt from the back of the rocking-chair.

She raised herself up on two elbows, eyes still heavy. 'Going out?'

'I've got a stage to catch.'

'Right.'

She seemed to be having difficulty concentrating, her forehead corrugated in thought. 'That's an odd gunbelt you're wearing.'

He glanced down needlessly; he knew what was there. 'I see it more like a utility belt, I guess.' Indicating each item in turn, he explained, 'A fork for polite dining, a knife, a double-pronged hook, a spike and a clamp. They tend to make my life easier from time to time.'

She swore, a fresh crease forming at the bridge of her crooked nose. Falling back on to the pillow, she covered her head with her hands. 'I ain't had that much whiskey in a long time!'

'Me neither.'

'What did I say?'

'Nothing you need be ashamed of, Jean. As Walt Whitman said, *Not till the sun excludes you do I exclude you.*'

She laughed. 'You and your books! I'll have you know I stopped being ashamed when I ended up at Ma Begley's!'

'Well, you can start again, if you like,' he said. He waved a vellum document and put it on the tallboy. 'I've been down and paid Mrs Begley. You're free to go.'

She stared at him. 'Go? Go where, Corbin? What with?'

He fished greenbacks out of his pocket. 'Here. It's only three hundred dollars, but it should be enough to set you up for a while.' He put the money on top of the paid-up contract.

'*Only* three hundred dollars?'

'I don't usually carry more than that amount.'

'No, Corbin, I'm just thinking, even now that's still a lot of money.' Moisture glistened in her eyes. 'Especially after what I did . . . '

'You were Sam's dupe, that's all. He's to blame, not you.'

Shaking her head, she whispered, 'I don't know, Corbin. I ain't so sure the guilt lies all with him.'

Taking his slouch hat off the dresser handle, he said, 'Forget the guilt. It's your life now, Jean. That money could make it worthwhile, worth living.' He shrugged and his hook moved involuntarily. 'It's up to you. Now I must go, I have a job to do.' He turned on his heel and reached for the door handle.

'Job?'

'Yes. I have business to attend to in Walkerville.'

★   ★   ★

The wide main street of Walkerville was patterned by the morning's shadows which were low and long. Even though his stomach grumbled for breakfast, Earl Woodbury rode his sorrel at a sedate canter. He was in no hurry as he approached the two storey building with its imposing entrance steps and large sash windows. In truth, he didn't dare ride any faster, else his tall stovepipe hat was liable to topple off his head of thick white hair. He'd been promising himself a haircut for weeks, since it had grown too long and appeared avuncular instead of business-like, but so far he'd never got round to it.

Wearing his best dark-blue silk coat and vest, complete with ochre cravat and silver tie-clip, he felt sure that this time Mrs Walker would look kindly on him. As she should, considering he had been one of the first permanent residents in Walkerville, though in those days it had been a collection of six shacks called Exley Creek after its mountain man founder, Goliath Exley.

Gradually, over the months and years, the number of dwellings and businesses increased. In his youthful enthusiasm Woodbury gathered the community together and arranged for newcomer surveyor William Denver to plan the town — mark off its streets and lots. Unfortunately, Denver had lost his surveying instruments in a storm, when he was almost washed away with his horse. Left only with a practised eye and a rope four rods long, Denver apportioned the future growth of Exley Creek. At the time Woodbury had scratched his head as he studied the town plans. It was only later — when it was too late — that he learned that Denver's piece of rope stretched in wet weather and shrank when dry, ultimately making a great number of oddly shaped lots. Still, it gave the growing town some distinction.

For his pains, Woodbury was voted in as the town's first mayor and since then nobody else fancied the job, so he was re-elected every time. Mayor Earl Woodbury — it had a certain ring to it. The ring of familiarity, he supposed, after all these years.

Vital lumber for building came from the mountainside and Exley Creek gained a sawmill in 1857. The following year the nearby hills offered up modest lodes of silver, drawing folk from north and south, even from as far off as Mexico and Canada. The silver mine's title deeds changed hands several times but now it was owned by Ignacio de la Fuente, whose saloon, El Dorado, rivalled the Watering Hole.

The town shrank during the Civil

61

War, as many of its able-bodied men were called up to fight for the Southern cause and never returned. As ill-luck would have it, the town nestled at the northern end of a Confederate State, not far from the borderline with its Union neighbour. Since the number of slaves working in the town and surrounding farms was about a hundred, the majority of folk often questioned why they were fighting the North over so few individuals. Others argued that they didn't want the Northerners telling them what to do, which Woodbury thought seemed much more reasonable grounds for their involvement in the conflict.

Times were hard during the war and even worse when the Confederate cause was lost. Mayor Woodbury was appalled over how such a thriving town deteriorated in the space of four or five years. Some false fronts were all that was left of many businesses: the buildings themselves had been used for firewood. About half of the slaves headed north, seeking a new life; others carried on working as before, though now they were freedmen; a few were free to become destitute and to starve. Much of the farmland had been burned or spoiled with Union salt. The taste of defeat was truly bitter.

When the Walkers came to Exley Creek in '66, it seemed that they were the answer to the town's prayer. Sure, they were Northerners, but they didn't carry carpetbags and didn't seem to belong to the interfering abolitionist cause either. They simply had money and were willing to spend it in the town. The Walkers quickly commissioned the building of a grand dwelling at the upper end of town, on a grassy knoll that overlooked the creek and had once been mooted as a good candidate for the cemetery.

The Walker residence boasted two storeys, eight rooms, besides a pantry, a china closet, hall, bathroom and four built-in closets. Its frame was imposing, raised five feet above the ground, with steps up to the veranda and tall double doors leading into the hall. But Mr Walker not only concentrated on building a fine dwelling for himself and his mother; he also financed a new schoolhouse and the renovation of the church. These two philanthropic gestures — the promise of a new era of reconstruction — endeared Walker to the entire township. The least they could do in return was to accede to his wishes and name the town after him.

Within a couple of years Walker bought up a number of businesses, including the failing saloon, the Watering Hole. He even made an offer for the silver mine but was politely turned down by Señor de la Fuente, the owner.

As Woodbury drew up his sorrel at the steps the double front doors opened and Mr Walker strode on to the veranda. 'Ah, Mayor, prompt as usual!' Walker's voice was thick and throaty, with a little hoarseness at the end of each sentence.

'I would never be so rude as to be

otherwise, Mr Walker,' Woodbury responded, allowing his mount's reins to be taken from him by a servant fully adorned in livery.

Ascending the steps, Woodbury felt all of his fifty-two years and was glad when he reached the level boards of the veranda. He held out his hand.

They shook briefly. Although Mr Walker was only about thirty — nobody knew the man's true age though the town dutifully celebrated their benefactor's birthday every year — Woodbury was surprised how elderly the man appeared. While the stoutness and barrel chest advertised a healthy man in his prime, Mr Walker's salt-and-pepper hair was thinning and he already carried evident signs of too many substantial meals. Indeed, Woodbury thought they were very alike, in stature and temperament. Save that Mr Walker had money and business acumen — and powerful associates.

Patting his own tautened vest, Woodbury said, 'I really appreciate your invitations to breakfast with you.'

Making a dismissive gesture with a hand, his host said, 'I wish it could be more frequent, Mr Mayor.'

Woodbury nodded and smiled. As he'd been addressed as 'Mr Mayor', it signified that the meal wasn't, after all, a social occasion but more inclined to business. Inwardly sighing at the prospect of not being able to honour Mr Walker's mother with his social graces and wit, Woodbury gritted his glistening white teeth and smiled.

'As you know, sir, I always have time for our town's greatest benefactor.'

* * *

Corbin Molina strode down the entrance steps of Heaven's Gateway and occasioned a few saucy looks from a handful of passing men; several women seemed to increase their pace and averted their eyes from him. It must be hell for them, he thought, the bordello standing in the middle of town. He wondered how long it would be before the council decided to evict Mae Begley. Though he didn't like her, he had found her reasonable when he bartered for Jean's freedom.

He hadn't been surprised to learn that Sam had arranged the whole thing. Sam had drugged Jean and carried her in his wagon to Mae Begley's back door. There, money and contracts changed hands, effectively selling Jean to the tender mercies of Retribution's bordello.

That was how Mrs Begley described it and Corbin had no reason to doubt her. 'That fellow Sam Buford seemed driven. Like he was in a trance. I tried a bit of banter — since it's no idle thing to sell off a human being, white or black. But he was single-minded. Just wanted my money. Jeannie didn't seem to figure in his emotions at all.'

That's rich, Corbin thought. With considerable difficulty, he kept his temper in check as he pointed out that her two brothers hadn't been particularly considerate with Jeannie's emotions either.

Mrs Begley's steely eyes latched on to

him, reminding him of a rattlesnake set to strike. Her voice deepening, she smiled without humour as she spoke: 'That's business, sir. Business is different. You don't let emotions muddy the waters of business transactions.'

Business in Walkerville called, he thought, and made his way to the stage depot.

While he signed for his luggage, he heard the doorbell rattle. He looked up.

Sheriff Deshler stood framed in the doorway. 'Good, I see you're true to your word.'

'Surely you've had no reason to doubt my word, Sheriff?'

'Nope.' The sheriff strode in and shook Corbin's hand. 'I hear you stayed all night at Ma Begley's.'

'Doubtless the whole town knows by now. I was visiting an old friend.'

'Yeah, right. I've heard it called some things in my time, but that ain't close!'

'Hey, Sheriff, why are you gassin' with that no-good low-down skunk?'

3

Behind Every Good Man

Both men turned to study the new-comer. The depot administrator made himself scarce in the back room, noisily rummaging among luggage, while the argumentative man stood in the door-way, arms folded. His clothes were torn and filthy; a draught through the entrance informed Corbin that the man could do with a bath, too. He'd seen enough hobos to know that beneath all that grime was a man years younger than he appeared; now, he looked about forty.

'Jeremiah Hood, I don't think you should be talking like that,' the sheriff said, hands out, mollifying.

'I'll talk how I darn well please! This ain't Walkerville, I'll have you know!'

As an aside over his shoulder,

Deshler whispered to Corbin, 'He was a drunk in Walkerville till their sheriff chucked him out. Can't get any sense out of the poor guy.'

While his attention was distracted, the sheriff didn't see Jeremiah pull a six-gun from inside his tattered shirt. Unsteadily, the hobo pointed the weapon at Corbin. 'I don't like the look of you!'

'Jeremiah,' Sheriff Deshler growled, 'don't be a fool!'

Evenly, raising his arms, Corbin said, 'I can't help my looks. It's nothing personal, Jeremiah.'

'Huh. If it ain't personal, how come you know my name, eh?'

'Sheriff Deshler just mentioned it.'

'Well, it's about time the sheriff minded his own business! Before you know it, the whole town council will know everybody's business and we won't be able to speak freely. Just like dadblamed Walkerville.' He waved the pistol about. 'Mark my words!'

Corbin noticed the sheriff easing his

hand towards his holster and stepped forward, hands raised. 'Hey, Jeremiah, I don't want a fight. Let's quieten down, eh?'

'Are you a coward?'

Corbin heard the sheriff swear under his breath. Doubtless the lawman had buried plenty of men who hadn't taken kindly to being called a coward.

Holding up his arm with the hook, he said, 'I lost my hand to one of our navy's shells, as it happens. One of the last battles, it was. I don't rightly reckon there were any cowards that day, on either side. A lot of needlessly dead men. Men and boys returning to their village burying ground, where they never dreamed of sleeping.'

The depot room went quiet.

Fumbling, Jeremiah pocketed his six-gun. 'Sorry, mister, I meant no offence. Sometimes,' Jeremiah explained, 'I get paid off not to fight, you know?'

Not to fight. Corbin recognized the guilt in Jeremiah's face. He eyed the big clock. Half an hour till the stage

71

departed. 'Jeremiah, I reckon you could do with a coffee.'

Nodding, the man said, 'I'd be honoured to drink with you, sir.'

Corbin tossed a coin over to the newly emerged stage administrator; he caught it left-handed. 'Load my luggage on to the stage, please. I'll be back at nine prompt.'

'Aye, sir. It's as good as done!'

Together, the hobo Jeremiah and Corbin Molina stepped out into the morning sun and headed for the café on the other side of the wide street.

Sheriff Deshler took off his hat and scratched the back of his head. 'That Jeremiah doesn't know how close he came to knocking on the gates of hell.'

★ ★ ★

Jeremiah sat nursing the mug of coffee in Mack's Snacks eatery. 'Hell, it's a hot day. Makes you feel as if you had washed yourself in molasses and water. I appreciate the coffee, mister . . .'

'The name's Molina, Corbin Molina.'

'OK, Corbin, thanks for the drink. Though my gut tells me I'd probably appreciate something a mite stronger.'

'I'm sure you would, but I suspect you're at a turning point in the road. You can carry on the way you're headed — or you can take a turn. A good turn, maybe.'

Squinting and cocking his head, Jeremiah said, 'You ain't one of those religious nuts, are you? Trying to buy my soul with a coffee?'

Corbin sat back and laughed. 'No. I think even the soul of a jumper is worth more than a coffee.'

Glaring, Jeremiah whispered, 'How'd you know?'

Corbin shrugged and sipped his drink. It was certainly strong; he had to admit it would taste better with the seasoning of whiskey. 'I've met a few bounty jumpers. But it wasn't your fault, was it?'

'Well, maybe not.' Jeremiah's face contorted in puzzlement. 'It's those dadblasted cormorants who're to blame, I reckon.'

Corbin nodded in sympathy. Cormorants were brokers who had provided substitutes for the draft — for a fee, naturally. 'The war's long gone, even if its effects are still with us,' said Corbin. 'As our late president said, it's a time for reconstruction.'

Slurping his coffee, Jeremiah sat back in his chair. His eyes had taken on a new lease of life. Maybe that was the potency of the coffee. Corbin wondered.

Jeremiah nodded at Corbin's hook. 'Considering how you came by your disability, you're taking it mighty well.'

'You're not to blame for this,' Corbin said, lifting the hook off the table. 'Nobody is, really. It was war.'

His thin lips curving in a smile, Jeremiah shook his head. 'Yeah, looks like you've got used to it. I heard about you; on the train, you was.'

'Word travels fast in this town.'

Chuckling, Jeremiah said, 'Tell me a

town where it don't!'

Turning serious, Corbin leaned across the table, his big hand forming a fist, knuckles up. 'What I'm going to say now is for your ears only, Jeremiah. Can you keep a promise to stay quiet?'

Jeremiah looked into Corbin's eyes and slowly nodded, as if mesmerized. 'Whatever you say, Corbin Molina, it don't pass my lips. I promise.'

'Here, take this,' Corbin said, sliding his right hand towards Jeremiah's.

Jeremiah gasped, taking the bunch of banknotes. He slid them under his own hand and into his vest pocket. When his eyes settled on Corbin's again, there was a slight hint of moisture at the lower rims.

Corbin settled back. 'I'm not buying your silence. That's to help you find the right road. You can either go on as you are and die in a gutter with your insides rotten with liquor, or you can take a new path. It's up to you.'

'OK.' Jeremiah gulped the last of his coffee. 'This is my tipple from now on,

Corbin Molina. But what's the promise I've got to keep?'

'A small thing. I'd like you to keep an eye out, so to speak.'

Jeremiah nodded. 'Tell me more. My eyes are your eyes.'

★ ★ ★

'Are they still there?' Martha Pike whispered as she sat on the wagon seat, shivering in her shawl. Jimmy was still asleep in the back among all of their worldly goods. Their night camp had been a dismal affair since Linus had insisted on not lighting a fire. The new day's sun offered warmth which was most welcome, but it didn't ease the chilling dread in her bones.

'You knew?' he whispered, surprised. The seat creaked under him.

'Of course I knew! You've been like a scalded cat on heat since we left. If we were going to a new life, I don't reckon you'd be so nervous. It's the old life we've left behind that's following us that's making you jittery!'

'Quiet, woman, I'm listening,' he said harshly, his tones low and concerned. He gripped his Henry rifle, minus the white flag, and eyed the trail behind them. 'I think maybe they're just making sure we don't turn towards town.'

'Well, then let's get going, Linus. I'll feel a mite better when we've put a lot more miles between us and Walkerville!'

He lowered the rifle to the footwell and patted her hand. 'It'll be all right, you'll see.' Taking the traces, he urged the horses forward.

★ ★ ★

Max urged the team of six horses forward, while his sidekick Lenny settled himself in the seat beside him. Right on time, the stagecoach pulled out from the depot, the top crammed with mailbags and an assortment of luggage.

Inside the carriage sat Corbin with

77

two fellow passengers. Introductions had been made since they accepted that they were going to be cooped up in this conveyance for the best part of two days. Sitting opposite Corbin was Joe Tillman, who appeared to be in his forties. His rig suggested he was a gunslinger. He wore dark worsted clothing and a ready smile beneath a thin black moustache. Sitting beside Tillman was a man of complete contrasts. Javier Jara wore a bright grey-and-blue jacket edged with gold lace, tight-fitting trousers and a frilly white shirt. He had a well-groomed pointed beard and down-drooping moustache. Jara's dark brown eyes twinkled with amusement as he related that he was going into partnership with his cousin, Ignacio. Neither Tillman nor Corbin divulged their business.

The journey was in the main tedious, leavened with intermittent bouts of conversation. The constant gusts of trail dust bursting past the leather curtains made breathing and talking a challenging combination. Most of the time, they concentrated only on breathing, and that with some difficulty.

Every ten miles or so, they changed horses and, brief though the stopovers were, the three passengers welcomed these breaks to stretch their legs and to breathe in air not clogged with dust.

★   ★   ★

About three hours after the stage left, Sheriff Deshler obeyed his grumbling stomach and eased out of his rocking chair at the front of his office. Leaning against the upright post, he peered across the street then swore. Food might have to wait. There was no mistaking the man who had emerged from the saloon. Arnie Granger.

Deshler drew his Colt, checked the cylinder was full and stepped down from the boardwalk. He had no intention of holstering his weapon but carried it by his side, against his right leg. He wasn't here to play fair, he was here to uphold the law.

Arnie shoved a rolled cigarette in his mouth and lit it, discarding the spent lucifer in the street.

'Excuse me, mister,' the sheriff said, walking closer, 'but you've just violated our town's ordinance by dropping that litter.'

'Litter — a match? You've gotta be joshing me!'

Deshler raised his pistol. 'No kidding, Arnie Granger. You're under arrest!'

Suddenly there was a deafening sound behind him and Deshler felt as though he'd been pounded on the back with an enormous boulder. The shock deprived him of breath and all sensation deserted his hands and legs. He tumbled forward, dropping his six-gun, but the pain in his back was so intense that he didn't notice the hard earth that rose up to meet him.

'Why'd you shoot him, Sis? It was only about darned litter.'

'Sometimes, Arnie, I wonder about you!' It was a woman's voice all right.

'He was just using the litter thing to get close!'

Sis? Curious, Deshler gritted his teeth against the all-consuming pain and moved a little so he could lie on his side.

A young woman in jeans and a red plaid shirt stood over him, aiming a smoking rifle at his heart.

'Where'd you spring from?' Deshler croaked.

Her big brown eyes looked him over playfully and he didn't like her scrutiny one bit. She reminded him of a cat with a mouse and he reckoned he was the mouse and she was planning on playing him to death.

She laughed and shook her head, auburn ponytail flicking. 'Heard the saying, *Behind every good man is a bad woman?*'

'Can't say as I've heard it put like that before.'

Her long face lit up. 'Well, that's me, Sheriff.' Then her eyes clouded and her facial expression froze. She jabbed the muzzle of the rifle into his chest. 'Who killed my brothers?'

'You're a Granger?' he asked, surprise catching his breath — or was that fear?

'I sure am, Sheriff. Stella, on account of me being a star in the Granger firmament.'

'The dodgers only mention three brothers,' he wheezed. 'No sister.'

'That's because I've lain low. I'm the brains of the outfit.'

'That's right enough, Sheriff,' Arnie chipped in.

'Beauty and brains — a deadly combination,' Deshler mused aloud.

'You said it, buster.' She kicked him in his left side and he gained some satisfaction from the fact that at least it hurt; so he wasn't dying just yet. Though, he thought sanguinely, death might not be long in coming.

'Now I'll ask again,' she persisted, 'who killed my brothers?'

Deshler bit back on the pain and growled, 'Go to hell!'

As if she suddenly decided that was the best place to send him, she stepped back a pace and aimed the rifle at his head.

Although he was tempted to close his eyes, Sheriff Deshler glared at her while he prayed.

'No need to kill him, Stella — a fella in the bar told me!'

She swung on her brother, snarling, 'Why didn't you say so?'

Arnie shrugged. 'Don't rightly know. Anyway, I think you should leave him. Shooting a sheriff's bad enough, but killing one isn't such a good idea either.'

'He has a point,' Deshler offered, his words a dry croak. His body was lathered in the sweat of fear. He was no stranger to the close proximity of death, but this was too close by far.

Stella Granger swivelled the weapon back to the sheriff. 'He paid the bounty on our two brothers!'

'It weren't his money, Sis. Let it go, will ya?'

'OK.' Lowering the rifle, she asked, 'Where we going?'

'The guy we want is called Molina, Corbin Molina.'

'What kinda name is that?'

'Mex, I reckon. Anyway, he's on the Walkerville stage — which left three hours ago.'

Stella giggled. 'Maybe we'll rob it as well.' Suddenly she clubbed Deshler on the head with the rifle butt. 'That's so he gets no ideas about chasing after us.'

4

In Walker's Pocket

'Where you headed, ma'am?' Jeremiah Hood enquired, glancing down from his chestnut.

Jean Pegram glanced up, her foot in the stirrup, one hand on the pommel and the other on the cantle. She was wearing a pale-yellow silk gown with wide bell sleeves held by tiny pearl buttons at the wrists. By contrast, her neckline was cut low at the throat and shoulders. None of her dresses was appropriate for travel, in fact. Her horse was loaded with two bulging valises, all her worldly goods. 'It's 'Miss', as you well know, Jeremiah.' He looked remarkably sober, she realized — and he was wearing fresh, possibly new, clothes. Most odd.

'Just being polite, miss.' He doffed his hat.

'I'm going to Walkerville, if you must know.' She heaved and swung up, lifting her leg over the valises and cantle, and revealing white dimity petticoats. Adjusting her skirts, she added, 'Why?'

'Does Ma Begley approve?' he asked.

'Are you her watchdog?'

'No, miss, but I don't want to see you getting into trouble.'

She patted her boned bodice; the papers and banknotes were next to her heart. 'I'm a free woman, Jeremiah. So, if you'll leave me be, I'll ride on out of town — something I should've done long ago.'

He drew his horse aside and then rode with her at a canter. 'It's a long ways to Walkerville. If you have no objection, I'd be honoured to escort you.'

She looked askance at him. 'Why?'

'I promised, miss.'

She smiled. 'Corbin, I guess.'

'Can't say.'

'Well, since you asked so nice, I'd appreciate your company, Jeremiah.'

They picked up the pace and were

soon out of town. He called across to her, 'I'd recommend we stay at the Crawford coach station rather than the Soddy, miss — food's much better — well, it's palatable, anyway.'

'You'd better call me Jean, I guess. 'Miss' gets awful tiresome!'

★ ★ ★

Mayor Woodbury licked his lips and with great reluctance declined a fourth helping of pancake, mangoes and syrup. 'Thank you kindly, Mrs Walker,' he said, his voice thick with a tendency to drawl, 'but I have to think of my poor horse!'

She flicked her linen serviette and giggled like a schoolgirl, which seemed to please Woodbury. Odd, she thought, what men take a fancy to: these Southerners seemed to like their women flighty and brainless, she surmised. Even though she'd never aspire to the magnolia blossom brand of charm and grace, she had no doubt she would be able to wrap him round her little finger, as usual, despite the fact that the besotted fool was about her age. She was amused to observe her son watching; before Woodbury's arrival he had declared he would take no part in the conversation but merely act as chaperon. Southern sensibilities and propriety should have been washed away with those rivers of blood, she thought.

Woodbury dabbed his serviette at his mouth and white square-cut beard. 'Now, then, ma'am, what do you want of me?'

Simple soul; she knew full well what *he* wanted of *her*. and that was never going to happen. 'I wish to speak to you because I know you are a man of gravity and held in the highest regard by the town council, Mayor Woodbury.'

Flattery always works. His rather sensual lips curled, showing small glistening white teeth which she thought were very much like her own. His deep-set nut-brown eyes sparkled, encouraging familiarity.

'Earl — call me Earl, ma'am.'

'Yes, of course, Earl.' He grinned and she smiled back but refrained from asking him to use her first name. Then she continued with her proposition: 'It occurred to me that our fine town is being taken advantage of, so to speak.' With regal poise, she stood up and her manservant moved the chair back.

She walked to the dining room's bay window, pulled the lace curtain aside and stared out. A fully laden wagon trundled along the road below the white-painted front gate and fence; in the wagon's wake ran deep ruts, each like a wound in her mind. Tarps covered the silver ore and two armed outriders and a shotgun guard protected the valuable load on its journey to the rail-head at Retribution. Why did wealth have such filthy origins? How she hated Mexicans!

'Taken advantage of, ma'am?' the mayor prompted.

She started out of her reverie, turned and nodded. 'Yes, Earl. You may have noticed. The mine's wagons cut up Main Street's hardpan. Our council is employed almost every day to repair the surface. It's quite treacherous for the ladies of the town.'

Wiping his mouth with his serviette, Woodbury said, 'That's true, ma'am.'

'Then there's the dust and grime from the mine itself — when the wind's blowing the wrong way.'

'I've noticed that, true enough, Mrs Walker. A darned nuisance, sometimes.'

'Well, I feel perhaps the town council should consider seeking compensation from the mine-owner. Perhaps they should levy charges against him? What do you think, Earl?'

'It sounds like a capital idea, Mrs Walker.'

She simpered. 'Capital, indeed, Earl!' She clapped her hands and offered the buffoon another smile. 'You have such a way with words — straight to the point. Capital.'

The mayor beamed, basking in her praise.

Mrs Walker's smile froze; she was satisfied and gave her son a glance. He too was smiling, though she suspected it was over something else, something secret and possibly sinister. Her heart glowed at the thought. She felt sure that the silver mine would soon be within their grasp.

★   ★   ★

Two Mexican mineworkers sat on the doctor's operating table. Dr Malinda Dix tied off the last of the bandages securing the splints to the younger man's broken forearm. 'That's it, Carlos.' She told him in Spanish not to move it for at least six weeks.

'*¿Seis semanas? ¡Aye madre mía!*'

'Me also?' his companion asked in halting English, holding up his bandaged wrist.

'I'm afraid so, Pablo.'

'But work — our wages?'

Her long delicate hands pushed aside a stray tendril of her burnt almond hair;

she really hadn't had time to tie it back adequately when Pablo and Carlos had been brought in. 'Señor Ignacio won't let you starve, I'm sure.'

'No, Doctor, perhaps not. It is a thing of pride, however.'

At that moment someone opened the door and then entered.

'Sorry to disturb you, Doc,' Sheriff Avery Clegg said in quite shrill tones. Malinda had been in the town now ten months and still hadn't gotten used to his voice. His complexion was always ruddy; at first she had thought he was just constantly embarrassed.

'Ah, Sheriff, I'm glad you came. These men were hurt in an explosion in the mine this morning.'

Clegg took off his hat; his sandy unkempt hair stuck out even further than his large protruding ears. 'That's why I'm here, Doc.' His compact short body, tending to corpulence, was at odds with the lean and hungry figures of the Mexican mine workers. 'Seems rumours have started already — some nonsense about sabotage. They're saying it's the freedmen wanting to organize a mineworkers' union, holding out for more pay.'

'Not so!' Pablo exclaimed.

'Easy,' Malinda said, holding the Mexican's arm. 'That's nonsense. Pablo, just tell the sheriff what happened.'

Pablo nodded. '*Sí, Doctora.*'

'Take your time, Pablo,' Clegg said. 'I'm all ears.' Which was an unfortunate observation, Malinda thought.

As they had done every day just after dawn, Pablo and Carlos went down the shaft to light up the lamps before the men arrived for work. They had only lit half a dozen when the explosion happened. They'd been lucky to get out alive.

Sheriff Clegg leaned close to Pablo, his wide-set sea-green eyes questing. 'See anyone suspicious?'

'No, *señor.*'

'Come on, Avery,' Malinda said. 'You know it had to be Walker's doing! He wants the mine as well as the town!'

Dour mouth turned down, Clegg

shook his head and said, 'I don't like the man, neither, but he's been good for our town.'

Flinging up her arms in despair, Malinda said, 'Is everybody in Walker's pocket?'

'No! I for one sure ain't.'

She exhaled and calmed down, conscious that she was distressing her patients. 'I'm glad to hear that, Sheriff.'

'That's as maybe, Doc, but bear in mind I uphold the law and don't go accusing folk without evidence.'

As she helped the two men down from the table, Malinda glanced over her shoulder. 'If you can't see any evidence in here, Sheriff Clegg, I suggest you leave.'

★ ★ ★

Leaving the mountain trail, Linus Pike urged his team of horses in the direction of the nearby Retribution trail.

'Is this such a good idea, Linus?'

Martha asked, sensing a somersaulting fear in her gut.

'I reckon.'

'But that Reed fellow, you said he told you to head for the mountains.'

Linus nodded and turned to face his wife. His warm brown eyes engulfed her, reminding her why she married this man. Despite the jug ears, he was considerate and charming. 'I thought about it a long while, dear. But I know for a fact that we'd freeze if we were caught without shelter at night in the mountains.'

'Maybe, Linus, but I'm still mighty concerned.'

He patted the Henry repeating rifle in the boot well. 'If any of them gets close, I'll deal with them, be assured, dear.'

He was a damned fine shot, she conceded, and had always put food on the table.

'Don't worry, dear. When we get to Retribution, I suspect that Sheriff Deshler will be able to help us.'

'I pray that you're right, Linus.' She peered at the trail behind them, but there was no discernible sign of anyone following.

★　★　★

Despite the hot sun, Arnie and Stella had been closing the ground between them and the stagecoach, but they'd had to press their horses to do so. It was mid-afternoon when they pulled in at the corral poles of the Grulla Station.

'Oh, tarnation, they've just left!' Arnie exclaimed, jerking a finger at the cloud of dust at the top of a scrubby rise about a mile ahead.

Stella lowered the bandanna from her face. 'I've been thinking, Arnie.' She punctuated her words with deep breaths of air. 'It would be best if we catch this Molina guy at night, when he isn't expecting it.'

Removing his hat and using the back of his hand to wipe sweat from his forehead, Arnie spat out a mouthful of dust. 'I reckon you make sense, Sis — as usual.'

'Let's rest the horses and eat.' She dismounted and led her horse to the water trough. She squinted at the veranda of the building on their left. A short woman was wiping her hands on the stained apron that was tied around her thick waist. 'I hope the station master's wife cooks better than she looks.'

★ ★ ★

Sheriff Deshler's reflection in the bedroom mirror did not please him. He looked awful. In fact he felt awful — his head throbbed without the benefit of good liquor in his stomach as compensation. A massive bruise blossomed on almost the entire right side of his face. His bare hairy chest was tightly bound by white bandages and he reckoned his complexion was more fitting for a morgue than here.

Doc Treadgold stood hunched over

the sideboard, washing his hands in the china basin. 'You've got to rest up, Ralph. That wound could easily tear open again.'

'Whatever you say, Doc.'

'I mean it.' The doctor dried his hands on a towel. 'How's the head?'

'Awful.' Deshler paused, then said, 'Can you do me a favour, Doc?'

'No, I won't be bringing you a bottle of whiskey!'

'That's a temptation, but that's not what I want right now.'

'What is it, Ralph?'

'Can you send a telegram for me to Walkerville?'

'Is that all? Sure. Who to?'

'A Mr Corbin Molina — the man with a hook. I need to warn him that Arnie and Stella Granger are gunning for him.'

Treadgold shook his head. 'Sometimes, Ralph, I wonder where our young country is going.'

'Pardon, Doc?'

'Guns may open up the country, but

at what cost? I've tended many a gunshot wound in my time — and then there was the recent unpleasantness, of course.'

A lot of folk hereabouts called the Civil War that. 'There's nothing wrong with a gun, Doc. It's the person carrying it you've got to worry about.'

'I suppose so.' Nodding, Treadgold picked up his medical bag. 'Well, I'll be off. I'll drop by the telegraph office.' He stopped at the door. 'Should I charge it to the sheriff's office account?'

'Sure. The town can pay.'

5

Lean Pickings

Dropping five dollars from his pay into the centre of the round table, Sheriff Avery Clegg held his playing cards close to his chest, convinced he had a good hand. While he waited for Smollett to raise or fold, he sat back in his chair, hat tipped over his brow. He was still smarting at the doctor's tone. Sure, she was concerned about her patients, even if they were only Mex workers. But it rankled.

He'd liked her from the first moment she came in on the stage and hung up her shingle. She was forthright, with a full rounded figure, firm waist and hips. Her eyes fascinated him, like autumn leaves in certain light. Despite her other womanly attributes, which were notice-able, he was drawn to her long delicate hands. Healing and tender hands: she'd patched up his bullet graze after that saloon shoot-out six months ago. Then he'd been real close to those lips — generous and thick: they were meant to be kissed, he thought. Yet they had scolded him in no uncertain terms.

He didn't have to wonder about her scorn, though he'd been denying the reality for months now. Three years ago, he'd celebrated his fortieth birthday and knew he was washed up. He was never going to amount to anything. At one time he'd planned on being somebody. Maybe not like Mr Walker. But somebody to look up to, somebody to admire. When he answered the advertisement for sheriff, he'd thought it was his chance. And it seemed that way, for a time. The town council was keen on his appointment and for some reason he always got the support of Mr Walker. Every election, he was voted in. He felt wanted — somebody at last.

That first week in April, when he'd only been in the job a couple of months, he'd been a little surprised to receive a visit from Rufus Begley.

'Hey, Sheriff. I've got a message from Mr Walker. Seems kinda urgent.'

'What can I do for him?'

'Says there's some important work for you — out of town.'

'Out of town?' Clegg repeated.

'Yeah, at Mr Walker's hunting cabin. A break-in, he heard.'

'Really? Anything stolen?'

'Don't rightly know, Sheriff. It was a ranch rider who noticed. Told Mr Walker right off.'

'What about the town, while I'm gone?'

Rufus smiled, showing gaps in his teeth. 'If you want to deputize me, I'd be amenable. Just till you get back from your investigations.'

'Well, I guess I'd better look see, since Mr Walker is the town's most important citizen.'

'Yeah, Sheriff. Will you swear me in, then?'

'Sure, why not?'

When he got to the hunting cabin Clegg found that the door was ajar. But instead of a ransacked place he found a table with a meal fit for a king laid out. With bottles of whiskey. A note said, simply, 'Sorry about the little ruse, Sheriff. Belated birthday wishes from those who appreciate you. Stay the night as my guest — but let it be our little secret.' It wasn't signed, but he knew it came from Mr Walker. The man obviously didn't want the rest of the town to get jealous about his favouritism.

When he returned the following day, Clegg's head felt like it was playing host to a chorus of hammers and anvils. As he rode past the hardware store, he looked askance at Sven Johansson, who was packing his chattels into a wagon. 'Hey, Sven, you leaving?' Then he noticed the black eye and serious bruising round the man's forehead and cheekbones. 'You been in a fight? Want to press charges?' He hoped not, since all he wanted was to drink gallons of coffee and sit quietly in the office with the sunshade down.

Johansson scowled and turned on his heel, lumbering back inside for more items to stack.

Clegg shrugged, which also hurt his head, and made his way to his office.

Over the months, it seemed as though he was invited to that cabin to celebrate more frequently. Part of him understood what was going on; after all, it wasn't difficult to put the pieces together. Usually, on his return the next day, a settler or a shopkeeper was packing up and leaving the county. Sometimes, the odd black eye and bruises were evident, but by then he never commented on them.

Of course, for most of the time Clegg upheld the law just fine. That was why he was shot up in the saloon — a cocky youngster accused him of cheating at seven up and drew his iron. Clegg wasn't too fast, but he was darned accurate. He got a graze, the youngster got a coffin.

'Fold,' said Smollett, which brought Clegg out of his reverie. He smiled, laid down his straight flush and raked in his winnings. A profitable morning's game. He eyed the wall clock: thirty minutes after noon. 'Sorry, fellers, I'm due to do my rounds. Better luck tomorrow.'

Smollett and the other two players grumbled and kicked back their chairs. Fortunately, the stakes weren't too high, so they didn't take it too personal. Shoving his winnings into two vest pockets, Sheriff Clegg straightened his hat and strode out through the Watering Hole's batwing doors, glad of his wide-brimmed hat to shield his eyes from the midday sun.

★　★　★

There had been little respite from the blazing sun for Linus Pike as he steered his team of horses along the trail that reflected the heat and the glare. Now, the shadows were welcome as they wound through a dry gulch, its huge

105

boulders rearing up on either side. The transition from mind-sapping high temperature to the cool shadows was marked by the sudden fresh outbreak of sweat. Linus closed his eyes for a moment of relief.

Martha gasped, her hand gripping Linus's forearm.

Eyes starting open, Linus felt his heart lurch and his bowels felt treacherously loose. Two riders appeared up ahead on the trail, emerging from a shadowy cleft on the left.

'End of the line, Pike.' Even though the man's face was in the shadow cast by his high-crowned grey Stetson, Linus knew who it was: McLaughlin in scuffed rough-out boots, faded Levis and a red-and-white checkered blouse. He recognized the other man as Scully, a mean piece of work, unshaven and uncouth.

'I don't understand,' Linus replied, his voice quavering with fear. 'Mr Walker's got everything.'

McLaughlin rested both hands on

the pommel and shook his head at Scully. 'See, that's what I mean.'

'Yeah, boss.' Scully spat on the ground.

Eyeing Linus, McLaughlin said, 'You go blabbing like that, folks will start to wondering about Mr Walker and his methods.'

'I won't say anything, honest, Mr McLaughlin!'

McLaughlin sighed. 'There you go again. Naming names.' He shook his head. 'It won't do.'

'I promise, I won't say anything about any of this. Me and my family just want to start over. All we want is peace and quiet.'

Smiling, McLaughlin said, 'Well, I can oblige you there — you won't be saying anything, that's for sure.' With shocking speed, he drew his revolver from its holster and shot Linus Pike in the mouth. Linus fell against his wife and she screamed, her whole body trembling, eyes wide and fearful.

'Quiet, woman!' McLaughlin shouted. 'Your stupid husband got what he wanted

— peace, eternal peace!'

Scully's laughter was cut short and he slowly raised his hands in the air as young Jimmy stood up in the rear of the wagon, struggling to heft the Henry repeater rifle. The boy's eyes were streaming tears as he clicked back the hammer.

'Easy, son,' said McLaughlin, raising his arms.

Martha Pike continued screaming, hugging her dead husband, oblivious of the blood on her clothes.

Suddenly, a volley of rifle shots echoed in the gulch and the boy danced and jerked as the bullets hit into him, thrusting him backwards on top of the family's possessions.

Two men stood at the top of the boulder on the right, Lloyd and Quinn, their rifles smoking.

In that instant, Martha Pike briefly re-entered reality and turned to look at her son's corpse. If her heart had been broken by the death of Linus, now her mind was shattered. She screamed, her mouth wide, the sound rebounding from the ancient stones.

'Stop that caterwauling, woman!' McLaughlin shouted, but she ignored him.

Slowly, methodically, all four men fired at her, taking their time. And the gulch echoed with the shots and the air was clogged with gun smoke and the stink of sudden death.

When Quinn and Lloyd had joined them, they all dismounted and ransacked the wagon.

'Lean pickings,' Scully said, scowling, as he flung the grandfather clock on to the trail.

'We get paid enough as it is,' McLaughlin replied. 'This is just to make it look like they got robbed.'

'Yeah, of course. Far enough away from Walkerville.'

As Lloyd flung a box of crockery to the ground, Scully whooped with joy. 'Hey, look at that!'

Money spilled out of the shattered teapot.

McLaughlin knelt down and collected the coins and notes then proceeded to share it among his men.

'Turns out more profitable than we thought, eh?' Scully said, winking.

'Leastways, it'll buy us enough drinks tonight in the Watering Hole.'

★   ★   ★

Soddy Station comprised a long sod-house with four rooms, one of which was usually set aside for female stagecoach travellers. There was the station master, his wife and the hostler. The main room held a long trestle table with three-legged stools arranged around it. The walls had been papered with pictures from 'A journal of civilization': *Harper's Weekly*, and the pages from a general store catalogue. A number of spittoons lined one wall.

Corbin thought that the food was passable for a dollar a head: hot biscuits and antelope steaks.

Javier Jara didn't seem to like it

much, hardly touching the steak. 'A little overdone for my taste,' he whispered to Corbin when the hefty station mistress was in the kitchen.

'I reckon the master's ex cowboy — they like their steaks well done.'

'Sacrilege, I tell you! I want to taste the flesh and its juices, not charcoal.'

Corbin smiled in agreement, then shrugged. He'd long ago learned to eat whatever was available and be glad of it. Food in the belly meant strength in the body, which might be useful in an unexpected and dire situation.

After the coffee Corbin excused himself from the company. 'I'm just going out for a stroll. Legs get a mite stiff, cooped up for so long.' All day in the stage and now to be stuck in here. He found the smoky atmosphere, not helped by the oppressive odour of the sod roof, too cloying.

A coyote howled, sounding quite close.

Lighting a cigar, Tillman said, 'Take care, Mr Molina, and don't stray too far. Some nasty critters out there.'

Corbin grinned and nodded. 'I'll keep close, don't worry, Mr Tillman.' He ducked under the lintel, shut the door behind him and breathed in the fresh night air.

Crickets chirruped, invisible and insistent, and thousands of stars winked in the black sky. Over to the right an array of cactus plants resembled men approaching in surrender, arms held high.

Fortunately, the wind was to the west so he didn't get the smell from the stables. He chided himself for being uncharitable; maybe they didn't muck out as often as they should, but these station masters did very well by their horses. Resting and feeding them and being ready at a moment's notice to replace an unexpected team. What must it have been like when this territory was still prey to raids by warriors on the warpath? Lonely and very isolated, even if the next station was only about ten miles off. Stagecoaches pulling in, pierced by arrows and more resembling porcupines than modes of transport; and then those stages that had never arrived, their carcasses littering the prairie. He withdrew his hat, transferred it to his double hook and wiped the inner brim with the heel of his right hand.

'You got your hat off because you're mourning, is that it, Mr Hookman?'

The voice came out of the darkness, to the left of the corral. It was followed by the jangle of spurs and the sound of a rifle being loaded. Corbin narrowed his eyes and stared. He could just make out the figure — tall, high-crowned hat, shoulders bunched as he aimed the weapon.

Slowly, Corbin placed his hat on his head. 'I'm not mourning anybody,' he said and immediately regretted his choice of words.

'Well, you *should*, you bastard!'

The report from the rifle seemed deafening in the stillness of the night; the bullet kicked up dirt at Corbin's feet.

His throat was suddenly very dry and his palms felt damp; not ideal for a quick draw, he reckoned. 'You seem upset. Do you know somebody who has died?'

'Yes — and so do you!' The next shot nearly took off the toecap of Corbin's boot. But in the same instant, he drew his Colt and fired where the muzzle flash had fleetingly lightened the darkness; the man hadn't had the sense to move.

In the same second that the rifleman yelped like a wounded cur, dropped his weapon and fell to the ground, another shot rang out behind Corbin.

Instinctively crouching down as he swerved round, Corbin aimed and just eased off his trigger finger in time.

Tillman stood on the veranda, his gun smoking. 'The kid tried shooting you in the back.' Over to the left, a slightly-built youth was bunched up in pain, his rifle lying on the ground.

'Obliged, Mr Tillman,' Corbin said, pushing his hat back with the tip of his pistol. 'Mighty fine shooting.'

'Don't mention it. I hope the boy is suitably grateful. In this light, I could easily have given him a mortal wound.'

Now that the shooting had stopped, everyone else came out from the station sodhouse. Corbin and Tillman strode over to their respective wounded attackers.

Corbin recognized the man immediately. 'I'll relieve you of that weapon, Arnie,' he said, gesturing with his Colt. Reluctantly, Arnie kicked the rifle in Corbin's direction. His left shoulder was bloody, but he'd live.

'Hey, Mr Molina,' Tillman called out, 'you're not going to believe this!'

'Just a moment.' Corbin helped Arnie to his feet, picked up the rifle and pushed his captive across the ground towards Tillman and the youth.

'This here is a girl, not a boy!' Tillman exclaimed, pushing Stella towards her brother.

Corbin noticed she was holding her right forearm; it was just a nick, but enough to make her drop the rifle. 'I'll say it again, Mr Tillman, mighty fine shooting.'

Levelling his Colt at the girl, he demanded, 'Now give me one good reason why I shouldn't plug you right now. Backshooters don't deserve a fair trial, even if you're a woman — so who in blazes are you?'

Despite her wound, she stood up straight, chest puffed out. 'I'm Stella Granger and proud of it.' She spat in his face.

'Oh, Sis, don't get him riled!'

After wiping his face with the back of his hand Corbin deftly brought it round and lightly slapped her cheek. Surprised, she backed against her brother. 'That's for trying to shoot me in the back, Miss Granger.'

Tillman grinned. 'Think yourself lucky he used the hand and not the hook, lass!'

She scowled at Tillman but when her eyes returned to Corbin, she gave him a predatory appraisal and her lips curved.

'I like tough men,' she whispered, licking her lower lip.

Pointedly ignoring her, Corbin said, 'I guess we'll have to take them with us to Walkerville.'

'I guess so.'

'Then they're the sheriff's problem.' Corbin glared at Stella Granger. 'He's going to have his hands full with that one!'

'I reckon so,' Tillman said, lips curling in amusement.

6

Cold Blooded Murder

The station mistress bandaged the wounds, then Corbin tied the Grangers' wrists together and secured them to one of the upright posts of the veranda. That was where they stayed for the rest of the night.

Breakfast was the same as the evening meal, so Javier closed his eyes and forced himself to swallow the central portion of the steak, 'the least damaged part,' he said. His eyes watered as he whispered to Corbin, 'I must suffer or starve. Only a fool starves if food is placed before him.'

Grinning in agreement, Corbin decided that he liked Señor Jara.

They all filled up the water canteens, then boarded the coach. Stella and Arnie were put inside, with Tillman and Javier guarding them. 'If they give you the slightest trouble, let me know,' Corbin said, 'then we'll remove their clothes and boots and leave them on the trail and send the sheriff to pick up what's left of them tomorrow.'

Stella gasped in shock. 'You wouldn't dare!'

'Just try me, Miss Granger.' His tone was husky and businesslike and he got no response. He slammed the door on them and heaved himself up top, among the luggage and mailbags.

Max the driver approached, pulling on his heavy buckskin gloves. 'All set?' he called to Lenny on the shotgun seat.

'Yeah, Max, all aboard!'

'Let's go then.' Max pulled himself up and released the brake lever.

The journey was as tiresome as the previous day's, at least until about noon, when Max slowed down. He glanced over his shoulder at Corbin. 'May be something up ahead,' he observed, pointing at six turkey-vultures circling.

Corbin levered the Winchester. 'Take it easy, Max.'

Almost sedately, the coach topped a rise and started moving into a shadowy gulch.

Up ahead, two horses stood in their traces, trying to shy away from three vultures that pecked at something in the back of the wagon.

'Poor bastards,' Lenny said, pointing his shotgun at the crumpled form of a woman on the ground.

Javier pulled the leather curtain back. 'Why have we stopped?'

'Looks like a family's been attacked up ahead,' Corbin called down. 'Pay no attention while I scare off the buzzards.'

Firing in the air, he chased away the scavengers. No point in killing any, he reckoned — the rest would stay around to feast on their brethren's corpses.

'Stay here, Max,' Corbin instructed, then climbed down. Opening the door, he ordered Stella and Arnie out.

'Tie them to the coach wheel for now,' he told Tillman.

Turning to Javier, he added, 'When he's done that, I'd appreciate it if you'd watch them while Tillman and I take a look at that wagon.'

'Of course, Señor Molina.'

As they both approached, Corbin studied the horse tracks. 'I'd reckon on four of them.'

'Me too. Look, this here's definitely something.' Tillman pointed at the distinctive horseshoe imprint.

While studying the impression, Corbin noticed a slight glint next to a small rock. He picked it up. A double eagle. He glanced at Tillman, raised an eyebrow.

Tillman shrugged. 'Maybe these unfortunate people had a lot of money to steal.'

Kneeling beside the dead woman, Corbin lifted her left hand and noticed a band on her finger. He turned her hand over. 'Look at this.' Tillman knelt beside him. 'She turned the diamond ring so the jewel was inwards, hidden by her clenched fist.'

'Here,' Tillman said, peeling back the woman's high-necked dress, 'what do you make of that?' It was an expensive-looking necklace.

'She must have feared robbery, yet she wasn't robbed.'

'Just shot to pieces,' Tillman said, shaking his head.

'It looks like they used her and the boy for target practice.' Corbin gritted his teeth. He'd seen more than enough death and he knew that he would never get used to it. Rarely had he seen such cold-blooded slaughter.

Tillman stood and took off his hat. 'We should bury these folks.'

'That would be the decent thing to do, but I reckon we need to see about these people getting some justice, not that it'll do them any good. We'll take them to Walkerville. That's the nearest town.'

Tillman sighed. 'What with the Grangers, the sheriff's going to be real busy.'

'True. That's his problem.'

They searched the private and household belongings but there was little worth salvaging. Things were either broken or smeared in blood. Corbin picked up the family Bible, its leather stained with the boy's blood. He opened the cover and the family name was scrawled on the front page, tracing the generations back some forty-five years. 'Their name's Pike,' he said.

Tillman retrieved a few letters and a couple of photographs in a battered old tin. 'Not much to show for their lives, is it?'

'Nope. Let's clear this stuff off to make way for the bodies.'

The Pikes' belongings were discarded at the side of the trail. Between them, Corbin and Tillman lifted the mother, father and son on to the back of the wagon, beside the family Bible and the tin of letters and photographs. A couple of blankets covered them.

'I'll drive the wagon,' Corbin said and climbed up into the seat. He set out ahead, the horses seeming to be glad to be moving again.

Tillman returned to the stagecoach and, once the Grangers were untied from the wheel and shoved back inside, Max the driver followed the wagon.

* * *

'Hey, Doc, do you want to go for some refreshment?' Avery Clegg leaned against the surgery's doorjamb, holding his hat. He smiled, his boot holding the door open.

Malinda Dix stood up at her desk. 'Don't you ever knock, Sheriff?'

'Sure, if I remember.'

'Do you require a consultation about your memory problems?'

'Eh? Gosh, no, ma'am. I'm sorry about that. I was just eager to get in here to see you.'

'You have a problem?'

'Well, yes, I do, Doc. I wondered if you'd like to join me since it's that time of day when folk usually eat and maybe drink something.'

She smiled. 'Yes, of course. I do get carried away with my work at times.'

'Well, do you care to join me at Sara's Eatery?'

'That depends.'

'On what, Doc?'

'On what's on the menu, I guess.'

It was Sara's own recipe — Steak Diablo. Ten minutes each side on the eatery skillet, then covered with onion and fresh jalapeños. 'I normally cook in flour,' Sara said, serving the pair of them, 'but you are both busy people and have no time, I know.'

The meal was surprisingly good. 'You know,' Clegg said, wiping his mouth with a serviette, 'this beats the hell out of playing cards!'

'I suppose I should be flattered, Sheriff.'

'Well, I didn't mean it to come out like that, Doc.' He hesitated, added, 'Can I call you Malinda?'

'No reason why not, I suppose, Avery.'

'Maybe we could do this another time?'

She let out a light laugh. 'Yes. After all, I have to eat.'

'You don't cook, then?'

'I can cook fine, Avery. Sometimes, though, there seems little point in cooking for one. Sara provides good and economical sustenance for me.'

'I'm due to do my rounds,' he said, standing up. He fished in his jeans pocket. 'I'll get the tab, Doc — er, Malinda.'

'Thanks, Avery. I'll pay next time.'

'No need.'

'I insist.'

'OK. I'll see you around.' He nodded, put on his hat and on his way to the door paid Sara. He stood a few moments, waiting for change, smiled at Malinda then left.

Sara crossed over and whispered, 'You want to be careful with that one, Doc, he's a mite possessive.'

'It's quite harmless, Sara. He's the town's lawman and I'm the doctor. Professionals just having a meal together, that's all.'

'If you say so,' Sara said, hurrying over to another customer who was waving for attention.

As she left the eatery, Malinda wondered about the sheriff's motives

— and her own. Of course, single women shouldn't encourage men's company, especially in public. She stopped on the boardwalk and watched the townspeople going about their business. The afternoon consignment of mine wagons trundled through Main Street, churning up the road. Children chased metal hoops, girls skipped, men rode through and women gossiped outside Tuttle's General Store. She spent all her time reading up in her textbooks or administering to the sick and needy, so had little opportunity to socialize. She swallowed, surprised at her own diagnosis: she was quite lonely and rather sad.

★　★　★

The sad procession drove into Walker-ville in the late afternoon. Corbin pulled in the wagon outside the sheriff's office. The shingle gave the lawman's name: Avery Clegg. Tying up the horses by a watertrough, he mounted the wooden steps to the boardwalk.

Sheriff Clegg stepped out of his office. 'Howdy, stranger. What brings you into town?'

Corbin indicated over his shoulder with his hook. The sheriff studied the vicious-looking implement, his brow creasing in thought.

'Bad news, Sheriff. In the back is the Pike family — '

'All of them? Little Jimmy?'

Corbin nodded. 'Cold-blooded murder.'

Clegg climbed down the steps, moved to the side of the wagon and lifted the blanket. His face drained white. Hastily replacing the material, he turned. 'Where'd you find them?'

'Along the trail, a good half a day out on the Retribution road.'

'I wonder why they were going there.'

'They were carrying most of their personal possessions — including a grandfather clock.'

The sheriff blinked, then eyed Corbin. 'Their farmstead's back away, about another half-day.'

'I see,' Corbin said, fearing that this assignment wasn't going to be a waste of time after all.

A couple of middle-aged ladies, wrapped in lace shawls, passed by on the walkway and averted their eyes once they comprehended what was in the back of the wagon. Were they showing respect or something else? Corbin heaved a sigh. It was becoming a habit, he opined, turning up at a town with corpses in tow.

An ornate two-horse carriage drew in alongside the stagecoach. Max the driver loaded luggage on to it and Javier Jara climbed up beside the carriage driver. He waved briefly and Corbin waved back.

'I see Señor Ignacio's sent transport for his cousin,' Sheriff Clegg observed. 'New investment for the mine, they reckon.'

The carriage drove off, its wheels bucking slightly over deep ruts in the hardpan.

At that moment Tillman approached, with the Granger siblings shuffling ahead of his pointed revolver. Tillman's face was set, eyes clouded, as if he was barely concealing powerful anger.

Clegg lifted his hat and scratched his head. 'Now what?'

Tillman said, 'This is Arnie Granger, Sheriff. He has a price on his head.'

Thwacking his thigh with his hat, Clegg exclaimed, 'Dadblast it!' He turned to Corbin. 'You must be Corbin Molina.'

'Yes. How'd you know?'

'The hook.'

'Of course,' Corbim said, still puzzled.

'I have a telegram for you, Mr Molina. From Sheriff Deshler.'

That explained it, Corbin realized.

Clegg hurried into his office and came out a few seconds later wafting two sheets of paper. 'Says here these two Grangers were gunning for you. Seems kinda academic now, huh?'

'Sheriff Deshler wasn't to know they planned to bush-whack me last night at Soddy Station.'

'Bushwhacked, you say?' Clegg studied the poster. 'The girl ain't wanted — '

'Damned certain I ain't,' Stella snapped. 'You've got no right to hold me against my will, Sheriff!'

Corbin shook his head. 'Sheriff, if it wasn't for Mr Tillman here, she'd have shot me in the back. I'll be pressing charges as soon as I get cleaned up, if that's all right with you?'

'Sure.' Clegg eyed the bandages. 'Do they need a sawbones?'

'Yes, I'm hurting awful bad!' Stella whispered, pulling a face.

'No, Sheriff, they're just fine. Flesh wounds, is all.'

Stella's face twisted, her eyes narrowing. She swore at Corbin.

'I reckon we should've bandaged her mouth,' Tillman said. He received a black look from Stella. 'Sheriff Clegg, is it OK if I give you a statement later? I have business at the other end of town.'

'Sure — Mr Tillman, is it?'

Tillman nodded.

'I'll lock up these felons, don't you worry.'

'Oh, I'm not worried,' Tillman said, turning on his heel and stalking down the middle of the street.

'What's eating him?' asked Sheriff Clegg.

'Don't know. But I owe him my life.'

'Looks like he's going to see Mr Walker.' Clegg puzzled over that fact for a few seconds, then said, 'Never mind him. Let's get these two miscreants behind bars then I'll go get the mortician for the Pikes.'

Corbin too wondered what business Tillman had with Mr Walker.

★ ★ ★

Sitting in an upholstered chair opposite Mr Walker, who was at his desk, Tillman rested his elbows on the arms and nursed a tumbler of bourbon and branch water. 'I am perplexed, Mr Walker.'

'In what way, Mr Tillman?' His protruding lips offered a smile but Tillman didn't believe it was anything but a facial movement and conveyed no emotional content. The man's lips were moist as he sipped his neat bourbon.

'I find that the job I was offered isn't

actually vacant yet.'

'Ah, yes. Let me make myself clear. Our Sheriff Clegg is no longer working to the town's benefit but rather for his own.' His whisper softened, conspiratorially. 'There are fears that he's actually pilfering the town's money.'

Tillman sipped his drink. 'Well, you hired him, so why don't you fire him?'

'That could prove embarrassing, since he knows a few things, if you get my drift?' He lifted a finger and tapped the side of his pug nose.

'I thought that might be the reason.'

'I want you to have a showdown with Clegg.'

Lowering his glass, Tillman let his free arm drape down the side of the chair. 'Showdown?'

'I hear you're fast. Prove it. If you outgun him, the job's yours.'

Tillman smiled, with irony rather than humour. 'You'll have to treble my fee.'

Walker's eyes widened.

'Sure, my gun's for hire, but getting

rid of your sheriff's going to need guile on my part — so it looks legal like. That doesn't come cheap.'

After a moment's consideration, Walker slowly nodded. 'Do it.' Abruptly, he stood up and strode round the desk. 'Once the mine's in the family's hands, I can afford to be magnanimous.'

Something told Tillman that he didn't particularly want to be the recipient of the Walkers' magnanimity. 'All right, it's a deal,' he said. Swallowing the rest of the bourbon, he put the glass on the desk.

They shook hands.

Tillman wanted to wipe his palm on his jacket in distaste. Still, the man's money was good. He picked up his hat on the way to the door.

In the open doorway, he turned. 'It'll take a few days to arrange, Mr Walker, so I'd appreciate it if you were patient.'

Walker nodded. Tillman put on his hat and left.

★   ★   ★

The town's two hotels were on opposite sides of the main street. Corbin left the stage depot and carried his bags up the wide steps and under the portico of the Happy Jack Hotel. Opening the tall glass-paned door, he entered to the accompaniment of a jangling bell. A young man in a dark blue outfit hurried across the carpeted foyer to relieve Corbin of his bags. He faltered only a second on noting the hook.

Sidling up to the registration counter, Corbin smiled at the pasty-faced desk clerk who didn't seem particularly bothered by a new client — or was it customer? — arriving. 'I think you have a room for me. Corbin Molina.'

At mention of Corbin's name, the clerk seemed to be revitalized. 'Of course, sir, right away, I have your key right here.' He handed it to the bellboy. 'Right, would you write — er, sign here, sir — right here.' He swivelled the register round.

'Right,' Corbin said, trying to keep a straight face. He'd be hard put to it not to call the man 'Mr Right'.

'Staying long, sir?' the clerk enquired.

Corbin signed with a flourish, pleased to note that he had been allocated room 416. 'Yes, a few weeks, at least, I reckon.'

'Right. Enjoy your stay, sir.'

'Thank you.'

The young man led Corbin up the wide carpeted stairs and seemed bushed by the time they reached the top floor. He lowered the bags and opened the door.

The room was well-appointed, with a separate washroom and a wide single bed. Light brown drapes over the windows seemed to emphasize the russet glare from the dying sun. The lad dumped the bags on the bed.

When he'd dismissed the bellboy he locked his room door and jammed a chair underneath the handle.

Corbin bunched his shoulders and stretched his arms; that bed looked real inviting. He unbuckled the straps of his leather suitcase and flung it open. He'd be glad to get washed and changed. He removed his hat, bandanna and shirt and strode into the washroom. The warm air was stifling, as he'd expected. Fortunately, the stagecoach hadn't been delayed. Corbin smiled: Major Newton's arrangements had fallen into place, as usual.

A large tin bath was filled with water and to the right was a cast-iron stove. He knelt down by the stove and opened the round door. Reaching in with his hook, he raked out on to a shovel four chunks of red-hot coals. He put these in the compartment at the base of the tin bath and shut the panel. The water wouldn't be hot, but it would be warm and soothing by the time he was ready to bathe.

Returning to the room, he unclipped the hook and fastened it on his belt. Then he unbuckled the harness and metal clamp on his stump. Glancing at the mirror, he noted a series of red welts made by the leather and metal. In a few minutes he was stripped and ready to step into the metal bath.

The coals had done their work. He bided his time, lathering soap over his muscular torso, and let the warm water ease the knots in his shoulder muscles.

Tomorrow it begins, he thought. He'd told the clerk he would be here a few weeks — at least. That was how long it usually took. Though in truth he had no way of knowing. It depended on the balance of power in the town.

When the bath water cooled, he stepped out, dried off on a towel and replaced the harness. Wearing fresh underwear, shirt and trousers, Corbin felt almost civilized again. He moved across the room and stood to one side of the window. He peeled back the curtain.

The room was well chosen, as he had expected. It offered an ideal vantage point over the full length of Main Street. To the right, an imposing private residence stood at the end of the street. To the far left lay the shanty town of Mexicans and their cantina, which they'd passed on the way in — The Mescal Button.

Opposite his window was the Presidential Hotel, quite beyond Corbin's salary and preference.

He blinked. Tillman was entering the hotel, as bold as you please. How come a gunslinger could afford to rest up in that place? Corbin let the curtain drop. He clipped a fork into the metal holder on his stump. The mystery of Tillman could wait. He was famished. He strapped on his gunbelt, moved the chair away from the door handle, opened the door and went down to the hotel restaurant.

7

A Damned Useful Tool

Stomach full with Chili de Sangre Anaranjada, Corbin read the local newspaper in the hotel lounge, allowing the beef and pork to digest. He had complimented the chef, a Swede by the moniker of Iwan Morelius. Apparently, Morelius had been on the staff of Baron Ernst Mattais Peter von Vegesack, who had been given leave to fight for the Union. While the baron returned to Sweden after the war, Morelius stayed and Mr Canaan, the hotel manager, was vociferously proud of his culinary acquisition.

After about an hour and two beers, Corbin felt his stomach was settled enough for him to venture outside.

When he entered the sheriff's office, Tillman was already there, leaning over a desk and writing on a sheet of paper. Tillman glanced up, smiled. 'Howdy, Mr Molina. Come to give the sheriff your statement?'

'Yes. You're way ahead of me, I reckon.'

'I find it difficult to rest in a strange place.'

'Even in so grand a place as the Presidential?'

Tillman's eyes narrowed. 'It's my curse, this eternal vigilance — but it has saved my life more than once.' He glanced down to the paper, finished writing and signed the statement. 'Here you are, Sheriff.'

'Thanks, Mr Tillman.' As the gun-slinger reached the door, Clegg added, 'Hope to see you at the game tomorrow morning — don't forget, eleven on the dot.'

Waving, Tillman said, 'I'll be there, Sheriff.'

'Game?' Corbin queried.

'Oh, just a friendly poker school. Most lunchtimes. When I'm not dining out with the Doc, that is.' He winked.

'I see. Well, do you want my statement, Sheriff?'

'Yes, please. And you want me to charge the Granger girl, is that it?'

'I do.'

'Well, you'll do for starters, I reckon. It seems Sheriff Deshler's queuing up to be next in line. She shot him in the back, or so his telegraph message says.'

Shaking his head, Corbin sighed. 'Is he going to be OK?'

Clegg nodded. 'Can't say, but if he can authorize a telegraph message, maybe he's going to pull through.'

'Let's hope so.'

'Yeah. And while we're at it, I'll pay you the bounty on Arnie Granger as well.'

'That belongs to Mr Tillman. If he hadn't acted, I'd be dead and Arnie would've gotten away.'

'That's what Mr Tillman said you'd say,' Clegg replied. 'He reckons it was your slug that winged the critter, so you got claim where he don't.'

'Well, I'm not going to argue. If Mr Tillman's reluctant to take the reward, then I'll have it. Maybe I can make good use of the money.'

'There's always our poker school over at the Watering Hole.'

Corbin laughed. 'No, thanks. I learned long ago, never gamble.'

'Yeah, maybe you're right. It'll be the death of me, one way or another, I reckon.'

★ ★ ★

As he crossed Main Street Tillman couldn't believe his luck. An ideal opportunity to get rid of Sheriff Clegg had presented itself so soon. However, he decided that he would simply play cards tomorrow, gauge the players and see how he could engineer a shoot-out. Maybe on the following day he could accuse Sheriff Clegg of cheating and finish it all with gunplay. The idea stuck in his craw, though. Manipulating the death of a lawman was something new

143

and not wholly palatable. He decided to visit the Watering Hole. He needed to wash away the taste of the deal he'd made with Walker, damn and blast the man.

Tillman spent a few hours nursing a bottle of whiskey. It was still almost full when he decided to leave. He'd seen enough. The frequenters of this saloon were harmless enough. Cowhands, farmers, shopkeepers and businessmen. None lingered too long. Nobody got drunk — probably the wrong time of the week. Maybe a pay-day was different; certainly, judging by the bullet holes in the walls, riotous behaviour was not uncommon. For a fleeting instant Tillman wondered why the town needed a sheriff at all. There were two reasons, he reckoned. One, they needed to feel protected against boisterous or even villainous outsiders. Two, they needed to keep the towns-people in their place. Yet Clegg didn't seem very well suited to perform the latter chore. Which was why Walker wanted Clegg replaced. From the odd snippets of gossip Tillman had over-heard, it appeared that their sheriff was usually out of town when any unpleas-antness happened.

Yet he'd learned that Walker didn't have it all his own way. No, the Mexican owner of the mine was flexing his muscles too. From all accounts, the difference was that Ignacio de la Fuente had acquired his additional property legally. Whispered questions lingered over the legitimacy of Walker's many acquisitions. A part of him admired Walker. He got things done. Fine, he was preying on a cowed and beaten Southern populace who had doubtless starved and struggled to survive the war. Was might right? Tillman reckoned it was — usually. At that point in his musings he decided he'd had enough. The smoke and stink of body odour combined to evict him. Since he'd paid for it, he took the whiskey with him. Might as well finish it off in the relative comfort of his hotel room. A fleeting image of Corbin Molina jumped into his mind — what was behind Molina's comment earlier this evening? Tillman smiled to himself as he pushed open the batwing doors. Naturally, Molina had been questioning the expense!

As he stepped on to the boardwalk Tillman stood quite still. On the other side of the street, the sheriff was striding alongside a woman and speaking in a loud voice. The woman was hurrying away, trying to ignore him. Tillman lowered the whiskey bottle to the boards, next to a wooden pillar, and continued watching.

* * *

'Come on, Malinda, you're single, I'm single, why can't we be good friends?' Clegg shrilled, reaching out and grabbing her arm.

Disappointed and annoyed, she swung round and slapped his cheek, the sound sharp. Her palm stung, as she'd hit his bristles. At the same instant as she turned she slipped on the steps leading down to the alleyway and over-balanced backwards.

Clegg's fierce grip on her upper arm prevented her stumbling and falling. His hold was hard and bruising, but it probably saved her from worse pain. He was quick, though, recovering from the incident and swirling her round. He dragged her into the shadows of the alley and pressed himself up against her. She felt soft and defenceless against his strong muscular body.

'Look, Malinda, you know you want it.'

She tried raising her knee to do him harm, but her skirt was taut, caught between the wall of the building as he pressed his slab thighs against her. Her shoulders hurt as the ridges of the wooden walls dug in.

'Hell, you're a doctor; you know a man's needs!'

He pulled her towards him, crushing her in a strong embrace. She panted with anxiety yet could barely breathe, her chest constricted by the weight of the man.

'I need you!'

The stubble on his chin rasped against her jaw and lips, hurtful, the sour-mash stink of liquor was almost overpowering. Before she could muster a scream, he pressed his lips against hers and she feared that she would suffocate. Better that than what he had planned, she thought irrationally.

The single report of a revolver was sudden and she wasn't sure if she heard it at the time or remembered it afterwards. The result was the same, regardless. Sheriff Avery Clegg's lips jerked away from hers. He half-shuffled, half-stumbled sideways away from her, the whites of his eyes glaring, almost accusing.

Even in the shadowy light Malinda noticed the blood at the sheriff's neck. And his head had been close, his lips on hers, when he was shot. Her instinct and training took over, submerging her trauma and fear. She crossed the small distance to Clegg as he sank to his knees then folded on to his side.

Her hand reached out, felt his neck and the sticky blood. Thank God, it wasn't pulsing out; it wasn't the carotid artery. She used the hem of her skirt to swab the wound, stanch it. Only then did she comprehend that a shot had been fired and the sound had resembled the report from a revolver. She jerked her head round as pounding feet thudded at the entrance to the alleyway. Several people stood there. Nobody seemed to know who had fired the shot.

'Help me, please!' she called. 'We need to carry him to my surgery. I have to remove the bullet in his throat!'

Nobody seemed inclined to move. Perhaps they were all in a state of shock; whispers and mumbling filled the air: words — 'bullet', 'throat', 'sheriff', 'poor bastard' and 'who?'

Abruptly standing up, her fists balled, she shouted, 'Help me now, damn you!'

Shaken out of their voyeuristic reverie by her vehemence and swearing, the crowd surged forward and four of them manhandled the stricken sheriff.

'Carefully now!' Lifting up her blood-stained skirts, she retrieved her keys from her reticule. 'I'll go ahead and open up!'

★ ★ ★

At breakfast in the hotel restaurant next morning, Corbin noticed several people talking animatedly, though he couldn't catch the subject of the topic. Since he was alone and a stranger, he was excluded from gossip.

After coffee and grits he left the hotel and turned left, strolling along the boardwalk past Sara's Eatery. He glanced through the window of Tremain's Barbershop; a rather corpulent man was getting his white hair clipped. He moved on and found the door to the sheriff's office open, so he walked in.

Then he froze in the doorway, staring in surprise.

Tillman sat with his feet up on the

desk. He smiled, showing tobacco-stained teeth. 'Howdy, Mr Molina.' He lowered his feet to the floor and stood up. A tin star was pinned to his chest. 'What can I do for you?'

'You're the sheriff? Where's Sheriff Clegg?'

'Seems he was shot last night.' He thumbed at next door, the barber's. 'The Mayor asked me to take over till things can be organized. On account of me helping to capture the Grangers, I guess.'

'Is Clegg going to be all right?'

'Too early to say. The doc was on hand, it seems, so he was lucky.'

Corbin nodded, remembering. 'I heard a shot last night and some commotion, but by the time I got my window open, there was nothing to see. A group was making its way towards the El Dorado. I thought it was just some cowpokes or miners letting off steam.'

'They actually went to the doc's surgery, next door to the saloon.'

'Who shot Clegg?'

Tillman levelled his gaze on Corbin and shook his head. 'Nobody knows.'

Corbin stood, hesitant.

'Did you have business with Sheriff Clegg or can I help — in my capacity as his temporary replacement?'

Smiling, Corbin said, 'I guess I'd better tell you. It's only professional courtesy.'

Sitting down at the desk, Tillman waved at a chair. 'Take a seat. Tell me all, Mr Molina.'

Corbin fished out the envelope, removed the official letter and handed it over. 'This will explain it.'

When he'd finished reading, Tillman eyed Corbin. 'Says here you're a special marshal. Under the protection of Major Gideon S Newton, the Head of the Ministry of the Interior Board of Reconstruction, no less. That's quite a mouthful.' He handed the letter back.

'True.' Corbin slid the letter into its envelope and put it in his jacket pocket. 'I've been working for him for about five years now.'

'Doing what, exactly? I mean, it says I've got to give you all reasonable aid at my disposal, which is fine by me, but it's mighty thin on what precisely you're doing here.'

Corbin nodded. 'You know as well as I that we Yankees started to flood the Southern states as soon as the war was over. Reformers, carpetbaggers, teachers, businessmen, some of them full of missionary ideals, plenty more just looking for easy pickings. The South was reeling, its businesses bust, its men exhausted or dead.'

'Sure. Many a plantation changed hands for piffling sums. I reckon it was a mite unsavoury, the hasty way they went about it.'

'Right. They'd have us believe that Northern know-how revitalized the moribund cotton industry.'

Tillman shrugged. 'If you say so. Where do you come in?'

'Major Newton's an old friend from the war. He heard I was in Washington on business and called me into his office.' He shook his head. 'Five years ago, in fact.'

★ ★ ★

Five years ago. 'Ah, Captain Molina, it's good to see you!' Newton's long whiskers were sprinkled with grey now, and the lines across his high forehead were more deeply furrowed, but he was still the same man in other respects. He stepped forward, limping slightly with his left leg, hand outstretched. The major's light blue eyes sparkled. 'Good of you to respond to my rather mysterious request.'

They shook hands and the office door closed behind Corbin. 'Your message said you needed my help, sir.'

Newton studied the hook, his eyes losing some of their sparkle. 'Getting along with it, are you?'

Corbin smiled. 'As if I was born with it, sir.'

'Good, good.' Newton was wearing civilian clothes, a smart grey frock coat,

154

a black waistcoat and a white pleated shirt. In an uneven motion, he scuttled round his broad desk and sat down. 'Sit, please sit, Captain.'

As he settled in the high-backed chair, Corbin said, 'I'm no longer in the army, sir.'

'I know. Old habits, just old habits.' Newton leaned over and opened a wooden box of cigars. 'Want one?'

'Sure, thanks.' Corbin picked up the thick cheroot and used the hook to slice off the end.

'My God, that's a damned useful tool!' Newton chortled. He struck a match and lit the cigar for Corbin.

Sucking in the heady smoke, Corbin nodded. 'I have an interesting set of them.' He lifted his jacket to reveal the belt.

'Yes, I can see you've adapted very well.'

'What can I do for you, sir? I'm rather busy administering our oil wells, but I'm willing to drop everything if you require my help.'

'Oil, eh? There's money in that, I hear.'

'Plenty, sir. Thanks to Mr Carnegie, I reckon.'

'Yes, I've heard of him. I thought his wealth came from the steel industry?'

'Partly, sir. He paid for a substitute because he felt he could do more at the home front in business.'

'Damned speculators! Don't you feel a tad sour about that? He was safe at home, making his millions while you were out fighting and liable to get killed?'

'No, sir. It was people like him who built up the strength of our forces through steel and weapons. The war might have lasted longer if he hadn't paid a substitute.'

The major nodded, then his brow creased in thought. 'As I recall, you were a three hundred dollar man, weren't you?'

'I was, sir, but I had no regrets. I didn't do too bad out of the war, in the end. All thanks to Mr Carnegie's

Columbia Oil Company — which I invested in straight after the war.'

'You invested, eh? I take it you did so wisely?'

'I certainly did, sir.' Corbin puffed on the cigar.

'So — don't get me wrong on this — you can't be bought, is that right?'

Smiling, Corbin said, 'No offence taken, Major. Even if I was bare-ass poor, I couldn't be bought. You know that, sir.'

Newton nodded. 'I do, I do.'

'Are you going to tell me why I'm here?'

Newton stood up and signed for Corbin to stay where he was. 'Let me pace while I talk.'

The limp grew more pronounced the longer the major strode back and forth over the dark blue and red carpet. 'Politics is a far dirtier occupation than war, Corbin Molina, be assured of that fact. Before he went, I spoke at length many times to President Johnson. He meant well but wasn't up to fighting the

157

Radical Republicans.'

'His Tennessee roots can't have helped, Major.'

'No, quite. Well, as you know, Congress overrode the President and passed the Civil Rights Act.'

'Must be three years ago now.'

'Yes. A noble bill, I thought — and so does President Grant, by the way. Established Negroes as American citizens and forbade discrimination against them.'

'But?' Corbin offered. 'Sounds like noble bills, good thoughts and the real world don't always see eye to eye.'

'Too darned right! Plenty of senators are unwilling to ratify the bill — and even those who went along with the concept of freedmen are reneging.'

'That's why I don't get involved in politics, Major. Trust is one of the first casualties.' He puffed on the cigar. 'I don't intend to now, either.'

'Fair enough, Corbin. I'm not asking you to go into politics. Your strengths lie elsewhere.'

'Where's that?'

'Somewhere where you can use your sense of fairness, your integrity and your stubbornness — '

'No need to get personal, Major.' Corbin gestured with his hook. 'I had no intention of lying down and dying.'

'Right, and that's why I want you as my special marshal.'

'Special in what way, Major?'

'You've heard of the Freedmen's Bureau?'

'Yes, they do good work, helping distressed refugees from the war. They aid freed slaves with medical help, education and employment.'

'A federal agency brought into being by Abe himself, God rest his soul. And since it was set up it has been hindered at every turn, and not only by former Confederates.'

'I'm not a medical man or a teacher, sir. How can I help refugees? Actually, we've got a fair number of freedmen working in the oil fields.'

'I don't want you to help refugees, as

such. I want you to root out unscrupulous and incompetent men and women who're hindering the Reconstruction. They're making it hard for the refugees, creating a south-north divide and, in truth, their antics are starting to hamstring the administration.'

'If I was to accept your offer, sir, where do you envisage I should start?'

Major Newton sat down at his desk, opened a drawer, extracted a brown folder and riffled through several sheets of paper. 'There's a town called Ashkelon.' He passed across two sheets of paper and a map. 'It's in the South, but carpet-baggers and the like have been robbing the few families and landowners blind. What with military law and all, they can't rightly fight back, so they just cave in. The Confederate survivors are becoming strangers in their own land. Northern businessmen are buying up or forcing out old firms and businesses. It isn't honourable, Corbin. Worse, it's making a mockery of the Reconstruction. It has to stop.'

Corbin scanned the pages. Tabulated columns of names, foreclosure dates, purchase fees. A great deal of money was involved. 'So I go in, make an assessment and write up a report, is that it?'

Major Newton grinned. 'Something like that. Serve justice. Show them the errors of their ways.'

Corbin placed the cigar stub in the major's ashtray, stood up and put the papers in his jacket pocket. Being the recipient of a certain injustice himself, he quite liked the sound of this mission. He smiled and held out his hand. 'I'll see what I can do, sir, and try it for a year.'

★　★　★

Five years ago, Corbin reflected. Since then the Bureau of Refugees had been terminated by Congress and white paramilitary organizations such as the White League and the Red Shirts had stirred up trouble. Other towns had followed Ashkelon, more than he would have thought possible. It was almost obscene, the way so many Northerners were profiteering on the backs of the honest decent indigenous population.

Tillman nodded. 'I heard about Ashkelon.' He pointed a finger at Corbin. 'Some folks said a town-tamer went through there, cleaned it out.'

'No, that's just a rumour. Town tamers use lead rather than persuasion and written reports. I'm just here in my capacity as special marshal for the Ministry of the Interior.'

Shaking his head, Tillman whistled and knuckled his hat off his brow. 'Well, I'll be damned. A town-tamer.'

Sighing resignedly, Corbin added, 'I thought it only right to drop in and inform Sheriff Clegg — but now I'm telling you in his stead.'

'Right. Well, as that piece of paper says, I'll give you any assistance I'm able. Count on it.'

They shook hands. 'Thanks. If you need to get in touch, I'm staying at The

Happy Jack, room 416. For the next couple of days I'll be going round the town, speaking to shopkeepers, asking questions.'

'Sure, you go ahead. Ask away.' Tillman paused, thoughtful. 'Do you think this town's like Ashkelon was, you know, dominated and corrupted?'

Corbin shook his head, smiled. 'Not every town in the South is suffering at the hands of greedy opportunists. I reckon maybe one in five sometimes needs a helping hand to see the light.'

'Sounds a mite religious to me, seeing the light.'

'You'd be surprised how certain powerful men take to religion when they discover how they've wronged their fellow men.'

Tillman's lips curved. 'I think your stay here might be real interesting, Mr Molina.'

8

Fort Fisher

First stop was Tuttle's General Store, almost directly opposite the sheriff's office. As it was a community meeting place and the centre of the town's gossip, it was always a good place to start.

The name over the entrance informed him that the proprietor was Sidney Tuttle. He spotted him wearing his brown apron, serving at the hardware counter.

The food counter was being taken care of by a woman near Sidney's age, presumably his wife. There were four customers milling around and two being served.

Corbin made a show of examining the shelves of tinned food to the woman's left. He listened to the chatter, most of which seemed to be about last night's shooting; though the whispers were rather hushed; he suspected that the customers were aware of a stranger in their midst and were being particularly reticent.

When the last hardware customer walked off with his purchase neatly wrapped in brown paper and tied with string, Corbin approached that counter. 'Mr Tuttle?' he enquired.

'Yes, what can I get you, sir?'

'Information, if you don't mind.' He held up his special marshal badge for a fleeting second.

Tuttle blanched and his eyes darted at his wife. 'I presume this is some kind of official business, Marshal?'

'Yes, but just call me Mr Molina. That'll do fine.'

'All right, Mr Molina. We'd better talk in the back. I'll just let my wife know I'm going to be away for a few minutes.' He glanced enquiringly.

Corbin nodded and smiled. 'A few minutes is all it will take, sir.'

Tuttle lifted the counter flap and hurried over to his wife. He whispered in her ear. She frowned as she eyed Corbin, then returned her attention to her next customer, who wanted four eggs.

Returning, Tuttle said, 'Follow me through, Mr Molina.' The flap was lowered, then Tuttle led them through into the back room, which was partly given over to storage and also served as a kitchen. Tuttle sat down at a small wooden table and indicated another ladder-backed chair. Corbin sat.

'What's this about?'

'Do you own this store?'

Taken aback by the directness of Corbin's question, Tuttle floundered for a second. Then he replied, 'Yes, outright, and we've been here fifteen years with no complaints. What is this all about, Mr Molina?'

'Ministry of the Interior survey. Nothing to worry you.'

'I don't have anything to worry about, sir.'

'Fine. Now tell me, Mr Tuttle, are you happy with the way this town is run?'

Tuttle's jaw dropped open.

'My husband has difficulty with some home truths, mister.' Mrs Tuttle stood in the doorway, arms folded. 'Sticks in his craw.'

'The — the store . . . ?' Tuttle stammered.

'I closed, told them to come back in half an hour.'

'You can't just shut the store! What will they think?'

'We're the only general store for miles, Sid. They need us as much as we need them. I told them we'd had some bad news in the family. They were most sympathetic.'

Sidney put his head in his hands.

Corbin got to his feet, offered Mrs Tuttle his chair.

'Name's Grace, by the way,' she said, taking the seat.

'Corbin Molina, special marshal.'

'Can I see your badge?'

'I've already seen it, honey.'

'Can I see your badge, Marshal?' she persisted.

'Sure.'

'He prefers to be known as Mr Molina.'

She eyed his badge. 'He can prefer all he wants. He gets Corbin from me — the damned fool's old enough to be my son, for landsakes!'

'Corbin's fine, ma'am.'

She pursed her lips then let them curve a little. 'Glad to hear it, Corbin. Now, what my sainted husband was unwilling to tell you is that for the last eight years our town has gotten worse.'

'Grace! Is this wise?'

'Wise, Sid? I don't know about wisdom, at my age. But I sure as hell know a few things. And I know that I don't want the Walkers to get away with it any more.'

'Walkers, ma'am?'

'They nigh on own the town.'

'No they don't! They don't own us!'

'No?' Grace Tuttle stood abruptly and glowered at her husband. 'Tell that to the Begleys, the thieving swine!'

'Is that Rufus and Mort Begley?'

Corbin enquired, wondering if Fate could be so kind.

She turned back to him and sat down. 'Yes. Why, do you know them?'

Corbin shook his head. 'No, just heard of them. Should I get to know them?'

She pursed her lips again and nodded. 'Maybe. You and them might have some interesting conversation.' She eyed his hook. 'But I don't reckon you'd be around much after. Those two brothers are not nice people.'

'Grace, stop it right now! You've said too much already!'

She raised a hand and tapped Corbin's chest. 'Are you a for-real Marshal? Can you arrest people.'

He nodded.

'Hang them?'

'Grace!'

'No, ma'am, that's a punishment that a judge decides, not me.'

She nodded. 'All right. I'll settle for that.'

'What're you settling for, Grace?'

169

Sidney pleaded.

'Marshal, I want to charge Rufus Begley with theft.'

'Grace, no, please don't do this!'

'Why didn't you go to Sheriff Clegg?'

She let out a mixture of a bark and a laugh. 'That idiot's usually out of town when anything awkward happens. He wouldn't go up against the Begley brothers.'

Corbin nodded and felt the old familiar tingle. This town was another Ashkelon, after all. 'Theft of what, ma'am, and when?'

★ ★ ★

Next, as always, was the barbershop, which probably was the male equivalent of the general store with regard to the town's centre of gossip. It was next to the sheriff's office and Corbin recalled Tillman's gesture and comment. 'Was the mayor in here earlier?' he asked as he sat in the barber's chair.

'Sure, stranger. You missed him by

about a half-hour. What do you want?'

'Information.'

'That's free, mister. But if you're sitting in my customers' chair, you get a haircut or maybe a shave, and that ain't free.'

'A shave will do me fine.'

Corbin was covered by a barber's cape. 'Name's Hank, what's yours, mister?'

'Corbin.'

'Don't you have a first name?'

The chair tipped back at an angle. 'That's it. No problem with that, have you?'

'None at all, Corbin,' Hank said, placing a small towel on Corbin's shoulder.

'I suspect I won't be able to talk much while you're using the razor.'

Hank sniggered, hastily lathering Corbin's chin. 'It ain't advised.'

'Well, before you start, tell me about your impressions of the town. Is it a good town, is it well run? Or do you have problems you'd like sorted?'

171

He'd used the same or similar questions in this situation before; invariably, the barber was amenable. Even when the town was rotten, the barber rarely reacted. Often, most things just passed these cut-throat razor-men by — after all, they listened to chatter all day, so once they'd mastered the art of turning a blind ear to it, it wasn't a great leap of imagination to become deaf *and blind* to unsavoury happenings that occurred around you. But Hank's hand acquired a tremor. Corbin wasn't too keen on that response to his questions. His hand came out from the cover and grasped Hank's wrist. The razor shook.

'Perhaps another time, Hank.'

He grabbed the small towel and wiped the foam from his chin. Then he pulled the cover away and with an effort eased himself up from the laid back position. He glanced around. There was only an old bewhiskered Mexican waiting, his greying hair unkempt; the man's tattered and dust-covered clothes suggested he might be a miner, though Corbin doubted whether Señor Ignacio would let a man off for a haircut. Worth the risk, he reckoned.

'If you have anything to say to me, Hank, you can reach me at room 416 in the Happy Jack.' He flashed his Marshal's badge.

Hank gasped and his eyes started. Slowly, he nodded, lowered the razor, and it clinked in the porcelain washbasin.

* * *

Not every town was lucky enough to have a resident doctor; whenever that was the case, it was always his next stop. Doctors knew much that went on in the town; they dealt with every stratum of society and learned a great deal from the gentle probing and systematic questioning of their patients. If a paranoid gunman was threatening your life and that of your family, you tended to show stress and strain — and the doctor needed to get to the source of your distress.

Striding out of the barbershop, Corbin placed his hat on his head, then strolled past the sheriff's office and the telegraph station.

He stepped down from the board-walk, crossed the alley entranceway, and ascended the next set of boardwalk steps. The next lot announced that it was the Doctor's Surgery. He glanced along the side alley. An external staircase climbed to a door and there was a window in the wall; maybe the doctor lived above his job.

His job? He corrected himself imme-diately on seeing the shingle dangling outside the surgery door. *M. Dix, M.D.* The left hand that he didn't possess twitched and tingled, as if his ghostly memories were its own.

★ ★ ★

Captain Corbin Molina had survived the hell of battlefields, of being half-deafened and suffering six or seven minor wounds and many mere grazes — fortunately none from the devastating high-calibre minié-balls — but this experience at the assault on Fort Fisher was something completely different.

At the briefing, Corbin learned that the commanders were determined not to repeat their failure of the first attempt against Fort Fisher in December. Now, as the second week of February approached, the Union fleet arrived off Federal Point. Corbin watched from the Cape Fear River side; all his men were in readiness. Everyone knew that the war was truly in its closing weeks. All of them wanted to survive these few days.

At 7.30 in the morning the New Ironsides, followed by the Monitors Saugus, Canonicue, Manadnock and Mahopac, sailed within 1,000 yards of the fort. Bravely, these vessels drew fire so they could target the fort. Within a short while the southern angle of Fort Fisher was devastated, its traverses literally disappearing under the onslaught.

The continuous sound was tumultuous and deafening. Smoke and screams from the injured in the fort filled the day.

Soon, soon, Corbin's men kept whispering but the night, punctuated by irregular bombardment from the iron-clads, rolled on without any orders for the land assault.

Waiting to attack scraped at the nerves and allowed those with imagination to fear one terrible fate after another; indeed, those without imagination didn't fare too well either, since most had seen comrades torn asunder by shell-splinters, minié-balls and sabre.

'It's the waiting that gets me, Captain Molina,' said Major Newton as he did his rounds.

'Yes, sir. Most of my war has been waiting or marching. Yet the time spent fighting seems to last for ever, even when it is a mere hour or two.'

'I know what you mean. You tend to live each second as if it was thirty minutes. Hard to explain unless you've experienced it, though. Your men, they're up to it?'

Corbin nodded. 'Yes, sir. They want an end to it all. I think we all feel that a victory here would seal the end, so to speak.'

'It may, it may.' Newton reached out, his gloved hand clasping Corbin's shoulder. 'I'll be with you when the assault comes, Captain. You seem to lead a charmed life so I reckon I'll stick near!'

'It will be an honour, Major.'

The waiting went on for another day, the bombardment unremitting. Corbin wondered whether there was anything left of the fort.

Finally, at 3 o'clock in the afternoon of 15 February, the order was given. Pain's coloured soldiers faced Wilmington while Ames's Division, with Corbin and his men, supported by 1,400 marines, advanced towards the fort. Major Newton was with them, to the fore: 'Onward, men, we're near the end at last!'

The men cheered, believing this

awful bloody struggle would soon be over and they could all go home to their loved ones.

The assault from the seaward side was an unmitigated disaster. Union troops were slaughtered in the surf. Corbin and his men attacked, hitting the fort at the west end through the sally-port. At a bloody cost, the abatis was scaled.

Standing on the rubble, Major Newton exclaimed, 'We've got them beaten, men!' He waved his sword.

Over to his right, Corbin watched through swirling smoke as colourful brigade flags were unfurled. Such a simple act, yet it heartened the men to persist. Victory was in sight.

Combat was hand-to-hand, bayonets cutting short young lives, as the fighting went on for at least an hour; Corbin and some of his men had surged so far into the fort, they were at the eastern end. Here the troops encountered seventeen traverses — bomb-proof structures, some sixty feet long, fifty feet wide, and twenty feet high. Between each traverse were two heavy guns, which Corbin's men spiked or captured.

'Now, men, the final surge!' exclaimed Major Newton.

Beside him, Corbin shouted, 'For the Union!'

Admiral Porter, his ship remarkably steady on a smooth sea, gave the orders to bombard the eastern portion of the fort and silence the heavy guns.

When the shells started to rain down, Corbin could hear them and sensed where they were going to hit. They made an eerie whistling sound, the closer they approached. His sixth sense urged him without thinking to leap towards the major. He managed to yell, 'Get down!' then the shell hit and exploded. Shrapnel and pulverized stone flew everywhere, but Corbin wasn't aware of anything, his world was black and empty of all sensation.

When he regained consciousness, he was lying in a cot in the hospital tent. His head throbbed and his entire body was in excruciating agony. Yet even so, he felt that the most acute pain seemed to emanate from his left arm, which was reluctant to respond. His right hand touched his forehead and came away sticky with blood. His blood-spattered tunic was pitted and torn by shrapnel and stone splinters. He heard someone groaning in the cot next to his and moved his neck, turned his head.

'Major,' he croaked, 'how are you feeling?' He found that the more he spoke, the more he expressed concern for someone else, awareness of his own pain diminished, if only slightly.

'Captain, thank God you've come back!'

'Come back, sir?'

'Maybe I shouldn't be telling you this, but while you were unconscious you were making terrible noises in your throat. The poor fellow on your other side reckoned it was the sound of you dying!'

Corbin turned his head to look at an empty cot.

'Poor fellow died.'

'Oh. I'm in a lot of pain. Haven't they got anything for the pain? Morphine or something.'

Newton forced a laugh. 'I'd settle for a brandy, actually.' He winced.

'Where are you wounded?'

'Thanks to you, Captain, it's only my leg . . . ' He glanced away, his eyes glistening. 'I'm sorry,' he murmured. Then he turned to face Corbin and lowered his gaze down to his arm.

Corbin was in too much pain to sit up. He tried raising his left arm and eventually he managed it, though the effort forced torrents of sweat out of him. He blinked and then groaned. His left hand wasn't there.

'I'm sorry, Captain, but I couldn't save your hand.' It was a woman's voice, soothing despite the terrible message it conveyed.

Through the tears of self-pity and pain, he glimpsed an apparition that had approached the other side of his cot. Using the back of his right hand, he cleared his vision. She was sloe-eyed but he couldn't determine her eye-colour because of the shadows here in the tent. She had a high forehead and a square chin and her burnt almond hair was tied back in a bun. Above her head hung a lantern casting a buttery glow, making her face almost ethereal.

In barely a whisper, Corbin said, *'This is the female form. A divine nimbus exhales from it from head to foot, It attracts with fierce undeniable attraction, I am drawn by its breath as if I were no more than a helpless vapor, all falls aside but myself and it.'*

'What in tarnation?'

'It's Whitman, Major,' said the ethereal female form. She held up a rather scorched dog-eared volume. 'The captain here is quoting from this book which actually saved his life.'

As she gently placed the book in his good hand, Corbin noticed that she had a strawberry birthmark on her left temple. His fingers traced the deep gouge in the cover of *Leaves of Grass*.

'This chunk of shrapnel was dug out

of your book, Captain,' she said, retrieving the shard from a metal dish. 'Fortunately, you kept the book over your heart.'

* * *

Heart pounding, Corbin opened the doctor's surgery door. Nobody was in the small narrow waiting room. At the other end was the door with a brass plate, indicating *Malinda Dix, M.D.*

A female patient opened the door and stepped out, closing the door after her. The woman smiled briefly from under her lace bonnet and departed in a swishing sound of dimity.

He steeled himself and knocked.

'Come in!' the doctor called.

He removed his hat and opened the door. She sat with her head bowed over the desk, writing up her patient's notes, and he glimpsed the back of her slender neck, the complexion reminding him of hay. Delicate shoulders belied the strength of those arms, he thought;

arms that could wield a surgical saw. Behind her desk was a single shelf crammed with books and above that a framed parchment sheet, a poem. He screwed up his eyes to read it. Yes, of course; it was *Another Spring* by Christina Rossetti.

'*I wish it were over the terrible pain, Pang after pang again and again,*' he said gently.

Suddenly, she lifted her head and her autumn leaf eyes lit up. 'Captain Corbin!' She stood, extending a hand across the desk. 'How good to see you! And quoting from her *Introspective*, too!'

He grinned as they shook. Her hand was warm, long and soft and his smothered it. He held it a second or so too long, then let go.

'Good to see you, Doc.'

She glanced over his shoulder; he didn't follow her gaze as he knew the waiting room was still empty. 'Are you a patient?' she asked.

'No, I'm just making enquiries.'

As if on impulse, she moved round

the desk and went through to the waiting room. 'It's almost lunchtime anyway, so I might as well put up a closed sign. It will serve. Would you like to join me and eat at Sara's place?'

He nodded. 'Wherever. First, though, I'd like to ask you a few questions, if I may?'

'Of course.' She returned and sat behind her desk. 'Take a seat, Captain.'

'I'm a civilian now, Doc.' He sat opposite her. 'Plain Mr.'

She eyed his hook. 'There's nothing plain about you, Corbin.'

He felt himself grinning like a fool. His heart had lifted on seeing her, but now it felt as if it was soaring. 'It's a surprise, finding you here.'

'Oh, yes, you're making enquiries, aren't you? So you didn't actually come to see me.'

'No. Normal routine, really, though meeting you is a very pleasant surprise.' He shrugged. 'I've seen the sheriff, the general store owners, the barber and now it's the doctor's turn.'

'Turn for what?' He recognized her tone of amusement. Her pearly white teeth showed as she smiled.

'I need to know what kind of town this is. Are people happy here? Or are they — '

'Downtrodden, victimized, that kind of thing?' she supplied.

'In a nutshell, precisely that kind of thing.'

'What if the people are not happy? What can you do about it?'

He produced his badge, handed it over, the touch of her skin electric to his senses. 'I have the authority to write a report to the Ministry of the Interior and in no time at all the situation will improve.'

'A magic wand, is that it?'

'Not quite.'

'Sorry, I'm being flippant.' A hand went up to the high distinctive bridge of her nose and she closed her eyes for a second. 'I just fear that you're only one man. Walker has several — maybe as many as eight — who wouldn't hesitate to get rid of you before you can write your report.'

'This Walker guy isn't particularly popular, is he?'

She laughed without humour and he realized that he wanted to see her laugh as he'd remembered when her eyes became mirthful crescents. 'Oh, he's popular enough. He buys his favours. In eight years he's done plenty for the town, and he doesn't let them forget it. The mayor runs the town council under orders from Walker. What Walker wants, Walker gets. Simple as that.'

'I hope you haven't crossed him, Malinda,' he said, concern in his voice.

'No, not really. He knows I have my uses. I stay out of politics — but I won't turn a blind eye if my patients are getting hurt.'

'Talking of patients, how's Sheriff Clegg?'

She frowned. 'He was lucky, I guess, if it was him the bullet was intended for . . .'

'I don't follow you.'

She explained what happened the previous night. 'Quite a few thoughts ran through my head when I eventually got to bed,' she said. 'Was I the intended victim? Was the shooter protecting me from Clegg's brutish advances? Did the shooter want him dead or just incapacitated? Questions like that.'

'A lot hangs off all those questions, Malinda.'

'And there are no easy answers.'

'The man seeking answers is the new sheriff, Tillman. Has he been to talk to you about last night?'

She nodded. 'Yes.' She pursed her thick, firm, rose-red lips. 'Despite the fact I could see he was a gunslinger by profession and he'd acquired the post mighty fast, I couldn't help but like the man.'

Corbin nodded. 'There's some mystery about him, I'm sure. But there's a side of him that makes me uncomfortable — as soon as he arrived in town, he went to see Walker.'

'He did?' She frowned. 'But there's another side to him, isn't there? I'm sure I detected it as well.'

'Yes. He saved my life on the trail.'

She smiled, cheeks dimpling. 'Well, I'm glad he did, Corbin.'

'Me too. Especially right now.'

Her eyes held a hint of yellow and glinted mischievously. 'Life can get complicated, can't it?'

'It sure can. Remember what I said nine years ago?'

She flushed and nodded but held his gaze.

'I meant it then and it still goes — once this Walker business is sorted, of course.'

'Of course,' she echoed, her voice turning quite sultry.

9

Questions, Questions....

It was always surprising how much ground he could cover in the first day. After lunch at Sara's Eatery, Malinda left him to go back to her surgery. The inner glow in his heart diminished slightly as she departed, but he consoled himself with the thought of seeing her again very soon. He crossed over to the cobbler's, Moyle's Leather Goods. The beanpole of a man running the place was noncommittal and only had good things to say about Mr and Mrs Walker.

'I've been working in this business nigh on twenty years and when I came to this town I heard there was this shop going vacant, I replied to the advertisement in the newspaper pretty darned pronto.' When he spoke, he didn't look at Corbin's face but at his boots. 'I had an interview with Mrs Walker and she agreed to give me a five year lease.' He pointed to Corbin's boots. 'You could do with a new pair, mister.'

'They're fine, thanks. Specially made.' True enough, his cobbler had strengthened loops put in the left-hand side of both; it made pulling them on easier with the hook.

'Suit yourself. Well, the Walkers were true to their word, and I've just renewed for another five years.'

He raised his head at last and glared through rimless eyeglasses. 'I don't hold with anyone bad-mouthing the Walkers — many of these folk even owe the shoes on their feet to the Walkers' generosity. I sure do, anyways.'

'Thanks for being so helpful,' Corbin said, turning on his heel.

So the cobbler was bought and paid for, including his soul, Corbin opined. As he left the shop, he glanced over his shoulder up the street towards the Walker residence. It was tempting to go there now, but he decided he needed a few more interviews first.

That familiar sixth sense tantalized his backbone as he peered at the two-storey building. He could have sworn that the upstairs drapes had been tweaked while he stood watching. He shrugged. Sometimes this job got you seeing ghosts and goblins in the shadows. Clearly, this was one of those times.

He moved down the street, past the general store, the Watering Hole and the stage depot, and turned into the wide-open doors of the livery stable. Invariably, the hostler got to know what made his town tick. He had to supply horses and buggies, feed and saddle-wear to the majority of the townspeople at one time or another.

'Hallo there!' Corbin called out as he stepped into the cool shade.

His eyes took a few seconds to adjust and, in that time, two men leapt out of the shadows and lunged at him. He was lifted by the force of their forward motion and landed heavily on his back, with both of them on top of him. Winded, he found that his arms were pinned down and one of the men set his weight on his thighs so he could barely move.

'Listen good, stranger, we don't take kindly to nosy parkers in our town!'

The man's forearm was pressing on Corbin's windpipe and he was having difficulty breathing. He gurgled a response.

'Hey, Scully, he can't answer, you're throttling him!'

'Well, maybe that's the best thing, get rid of him for good and all!'

'I thought we was to scare him off, not kill him?'

'For crying out loud, Quinn, these types never scare easy!'

Corbin took advantage of their distraction with the conversation and sensed an easing of Quinn's weight on his legs. Just enough. He tensed and heaved, his powerful thigh muscles straining, and his buttocks digging into the earth. Quinn yelped and half-stumbled, half leapt into the back of Scully, who was kneeling on Corbin's arms.

Scully lost his balance and see-sawed, just enough for Corbin to move his left arm out from under and slam the hook hard into Scully's side. The man screamed and fell over, jerking in pain on the livery floor.

In the next second, Corbin rolled away in the other direction and got to his knees, then his feet. His right arm was slightly numb but his left functioned just fine, as it was used to pain and mistreatment. He clamped the hook on a pitchfork which he then transferred to his good hand.

Quinn struggled to his feet and backed away. 'Hey, mister, no need to get riled. We was following orders, is all!'

'Quiet, you idiot!' snarled Scully, painfully getting to his feet, one hand nursing the wound in his side.

When Scully reached for his six-gun,

Corbin was ready. In the blinking of an eye he dropped the pitchfork, cleared leather and fired a single shot, shattering Scully's shoulder. Then he levelled the weapon on Quinn. 'Stay right where you are, Quinn.'

'How'd you know my name?' Quinn bleated.

'Jeezus, you're dense!' wheezed Scully as he leaned against a horse stall.

'Both of you are under arrest,' said Sheriff Tillman, his silhouette appearing in the entrance.

'Oh, hell!' moaned Scully.

'Glad you could make it,' Corbin said. 'Saves me the trip to your office and jail.' A sudden thought struck him. 'I suppose you've got room for these two?'

Tillman grinned. 'Oh, I've got room. And room to spare.' He waved his revolver at the two men and they moved gingerly towards the lawman. 'I have a feeling that before long it may get a tad overcrowded in there. But I'll worry about that if it happens.'

Corbin gestured at the livery man, who only now emerged from the shadows at the other end of the building. 'I have a few questions for this fellow,' he said. 'OK if I catch up with you later?'

'No problem,' said Tillman, relieving his captives of their weapons. 'I know where you're staying.'

* * *

The liveryman, Walter, proved helpful. He'd seen the gradual erosion of the old town community and in its place was something that in his view stank to high heaven. 'The Walkers made me an offer, but I turned them down flat. I'd worked this place for ten years, I wasn't having any newcomer taking over — and for peanuts at that.' He nursed a bruised eye. 'Glad the new sheriff's arrested those two fellas, Mr Molina, I reckon I might press charges against that Scully — he did this.'

'What did Scully want?'

'Scare me off. Same as with you, I guess.'

'Why scare you off? The town still needs a livery business.'

'That's what I told them. Who's got the expertise, eh, tell me that? They laughed, said they could bring in someone cheap who'd do as they wanted and ask no awkward questions.'

'What questions have you asked, Walter?'

'Time to time, I've seen markings on the Walker horses. Good horses — thoroughbreds — but the brands ain't genuine.' He rubbed his chin ruefully. 'I guess I should've kept quiet.'

'Not if you want to sleep at night, Walter.'

'Sure, that's what I thought.' He grinned and showed two teeth missing. Corbin wondered if that deficiency was thanks to Scully too.

'Can I count on your comments when I write my report?'

'You sure can, Marshal Molina.'

They shook hands and Corbin

197

stepped out into blazing sunlight.

Next to the livery were several ramshackle dwellings. A painted sign on the boardwalk showed white paint on black, *Freedmen*.

Corbin paused and glanced over to his left. On the other side of the street, next to the El Dorado saloon, was a similar collection of hovels. The sign there said in red paint, *Mexes*. Real sociable town, he opined. Further down was the cantina.

He turned back to the freedmen section of Walkerville; they didn't appear to have a cantina, saloon or alternative.

Once it was established that he had fought for the Union, several freed women stepped forward and were willing to speak to him. But he didn't get very far. In truth, few towns were going to be kind to them, and they knew it. Was Walkerville worse than most? They didn't rightly know. Even so many years after the conflict, freedom was still quite new to them, so what it was supposed to feel like wasn't really understood. Missionaries and abolitionists said that the colour of a person's skin didn't matter, but in the real world it seemed that it did. So whom did they believe?

For about two hours Corbin talked to the black women and old decrepit men, all of them freed slaves. The able-bodied men were away at the silver mine. If he had questions which needed answering, then he would have to come back in the evening, when the men returned. The elders were reluctant to talk at all. Corbin sympathized; their familiar world had been turned upside down and what they had known — whether that was good or bad — was no more.

Bidding a couple of women *adios*, he crossed the street to the Mexican quarter. Here, he suspected that he would be viewed with suspicion because he was a Yankee — and, worse, he was only half-Mexican.

He stepped up on to the boardwalk

and strolled past four closed doors. He could hear voices inside these homes, but they were all female or children. He guessed that the men would be at the mine too. There wasn't much alternative work, after all. He'd noticed some buildings being erected on the west side of town, behind Main Street. Maybe a few Mexicans and freedmen worked there. He'd check it out tomorrow.

For now, he decided on visiting the cantina, the Mescal Button. He swung open the creaking batwings and the deep murmur of the dozen men at the bar ceased abruptly. Clearly, not all of the men worked in the mine. The shady coolness was welcome, even if the clientele was anything but. Leaning on the bar, he ordered a beer and tequila. He'd found the beer in these parts a tad too yeasty so the liquor should mitigate the taste.

'Sure, gringo. Though you will have to wait.'

Corbin glanced down the bar. Two men were propped up against it at the far end, supping contentedly; the remainder of the clientele sat at tables. The chatter started up again, lower in volume now; everybody seemed to be interested in anything and anywhere but the bar counter. 'How long must I wait, barkeep?'

'Until I feel it is time to serve you, señor.' He used a cloth to wipe an already dry glass then eyed the clock on the wall opposite. He shrugged. 'You might wait less at the El Dorado, señor.'

'Are you this unfriendly to all gringo customers, or are you just having a bad day?'

'Unfriendly, señor? I said I would bring your drink. You must be patient, that is all.'

'I'm here to ask a few questions, barkeep. Asking questions makes me thirsty.'

The barman shrugged. 'Then slake your thirst elsewhere. I do not answer questions of gringo strangers.'

The batwings creaked again. 'Pepe, I

think you should answer this man's questions politely — and give him his drink!'

Slowly turning, Corbin recognized Javier Jara in the doorway. He grinned and waved his hook.

'*Sí*, Señor Jara,' Pepe the barkeep responded. 'At once!'

His order was placed in front of Corbin with alacrity — and he noticed that the glasses were sparkling clean.

As he put down another full glass for Javier, the barman leaned across to Corbin and said, 'You should have said you're a friend of Señor Jara!'

'Clearly.'

Corbin turned and shook Javier's hand.

'I'm curious, Mr Molina.' Javier's dark brown eyes sparkled. 'What questions are you asking here?'

Pulling out his badge, Corbin explained, 'The Ministry of the Interior has received reports that suggest the original townspeople are being robbed of their livelihood by the corrupt administration.'

Javier stroked his pointed beard and

down-drooping moustache. 'I have just come from my cousin's hacienda and he says the same thing. But his men are not gunfighters, while Walker's are, most decidedly.'

'And Walker is putting pressure on him to sell the mine, isn't he?'

'Yes. Yesterday's explosion is the most recent attempt at persuasion. But of course there is no proof against the man.'

'If you don't mind me asking, Señor Jara, why did you come to Walkerville?'

Javier sipped his drink. 'I have money to spare. I offer it to my cousin for two purposes. First, he still uses the patio process to recover the silver from the ore; this takes weeks. I say to him, he should use the *fondo* process, since it takes only fifteen or so hours.'

'That's a big saving in process time, *señor*.'

'*Sí*. Ignacio, he is stuck in his ways. It is the same with his pride. He uses only men close to him to protect his mine. I say, he should hire gunmen. I pay, I say.

Seven good guns would rid the town of these evil men. I try to convince him it is the only way.'

'Sometimes, it is. Other times, the gunmen simply replace those they've gunned down and take over the town. I've known it happen.'

'I had not thought of that. It must be difficult to find gunmen you can trust, no?'

'That can be a problem, yes.' The tequila hit the spot and made way for the warm beer which was anything but refreshing.

'I don't suppose you'd like to come out to see my cousin?'

'Sure. Tomorrow — at ten?'

Javier nodded. 'I will tell him. He will send the carriage for you.'

'That's decent of him.'

Shaking hands, they left together.

★ ★ ★

Shaking the jail bars to no avail, Quinn said, 'Angus, you've got to get us out of here! Tell Mr Walker. He'll soon talk the sheriff into letting us go!'

Arms akimbo, McLaughlin stood and surveyed Quinn and the supine form of Scully whose torso was all bandaged up. His gunbelt was empty, as he'd left the weapon with the sheriff in the office. Behind him, in brooding silence sat Arnie and Stella Granger in their separate cells.

McLaughlin sighed. 'If I've told you once, I've told you a dozen times, don't go thinking for yourselves, the pair of you!'

'We heard from Hank, he said the guy was nosing around where he shouldn't. We thought we'd scare him off, Angus, that's all.' Quinn squinted. 'I mean, he's only got one hand.'

'Yeah, but he's mighty fast on the draw,' added Scully.

Quinn turned to Scully. 'See that bandage, Angus?'

'Yes, what of it?'

'That guy almost ripped out Scully's guts with his hook!'

'Yeah, it sure as hell hurt, but I reckon without his hook he'd be easy to take.'

McLaughlin smirked. 'I thought you said he was fast?'

'Yeah, but I'd been almost 'viscerated and was hurtin' bad at the time. In a fair gunfight, I could take him. Easy.'

'Who wants to be in a fair gunfight?' McLaughlin demanded, and all three laughed.

Then McLaughlin's face turned serious again. 'I'll speak to Mr Walker.' He leaned close to the bars and whispered, 'We don't rightly know what to make of the new sheriff yet.'

'Well, he got rid of Clegg, didn't he?'

'Seems like. But he hasn't been back to report to Mr Walker since.'

'I reckon he's playing it cagey,' whispered Quinn. 'It'd look mighty suspicious, him running off to Mr Walker straight after he takes over as sheriff.'

McLaughlin rasped a hand over his chin. 'You surprise me, sometimes,

Quinn. You really do.'

'Thanks, Angus.'

*   *   *

'Angus, what you say gives me great concern,' said Mrs Walker as she paced past the window of the library. She glanced across at her son, who sat at the desk and seemed to be taking the news rather equably. 'Great concern indeed.'

'Yes, ma'am,' McLaughlin said, standing with his hat in his hands.

She paused and swung on the foreman. 'Do you know who this man has questioned?'

Scratching his ear lobe, McLaughlin said, 'Couldn't say for sure who, exactly, ma'am. For certain, Hank Tremain the barber and Moyle, the cobbler — who, I might add, gave glowing references to — '

'References! *References for us?*'

Wishing he hadn't phrased it quite like that, McLaughlin hurriedly added, 'I think he also went to the Tuttles.'

207

'The Tuttles, damn them,' she murmured, 'if they weren't so good at stock-taking, I'd have had them out ages ago.'

'Why all the concern, Ma?'

'Because, son, if an outsider is asking questions, he's doing it at the behest of another outsider — which means trouble for us, make no mistake!'

'He's only one man, Mrs Walker,' said McLaughlin.

'Maybe he is, but I'm more troubled about what he did to Scully and Quinn.'

McLaughlin nodded but kept silent.

Exasperated, Mrs Walker let out a gasp. 'Let them stew in the sheriff's jail for a while — serves them right, the imbeciles!'

'What about the man who's asking questions, Ma?'

She nodded at her son then turned to McLaughlin. 'Run him out of town, Angus. Hear me? Run him out!'

Walker said, 'Sounds like it's time for the new sheriff to turn a blind eye, eh?'

'Precisely,' his mother snapped.

Moving awkwardly from one foot to

the other, McLaughlin said, 'The man's mean, as Scully can vouch for, ma'am. What if he has no mind to leave town?'

'His mind is of no consequence to me, Angus. His presence in our town is, however. Persuade him and if that fails — well, there are plenty dry gulches on the way to Retribution . . .'

'Right, ma'am,' said McLaughlin. 'I'll see to it.' He nodded to the pair of them, turned on his heel and opened the library door. On his way into the vestibule he donned his hat.

As soon as their foreman had left and closed the door, Lydia Walker said, 'This business with the stranger mustn't interfere with our plans for the mine, son.'

Walker stood up, strode round the desk and hugged his mother briefly. 'I know that, Ma. But I don't see how your idea to get the mayor to raise taxes against the mining company is going to help us — it'll take months for the taxes to hurt.'

'Until Angus told me about the

stranger asking questions, I thought we had plenty of time to play a long game.'

'But now?'

'Now, son, we need to act. But let the taxes argument go ahead anyway. Let them know it came from us. That way, we're less likely to be suspected, we're seen to be employing commercial chicanery — which is acceptable — and not violence.'

'But we *are* going to use violence, aren't we, Ma?'

'Yes, but no more explosions in the mine, my dear. We want it in one piece, don't we?' She patted his cheek and smiled. 'I think two of your men would be sufficient to persuade the Mexicans of this town to quit and go elsewhere. Without most of his labour force, the señor will give up.'

'You sure don't like Mexicans, Ma.'

'No, I don't, son — and with good reason.' She made a barking laugh. 'I'd prefer freedmen any day.'

★ ★ ★

Corbin returned to the freedmen's hovels and met two tall muscular men. Amos and Saul were happy enough, it seemed. 'We're glad of the work, Marshal,' said Amos. 'The Mexican, Señor Ignacio, he doesn't pay so good, but he's fair.'

'As for the town,' said Saul, 'let us be truthful here, Walker runs the town.'

'Aye,' agreed Amos, 'he bought his way in. Paid for a school and a church. But our children can't attend the school. Walker got the council to sack the two teachers from the north who wanted to teach our children. He seems to be against education where our children are concerned.'

'Yet,' added Saul, 'he built the church.'

'Hypocrite,' concluded Amos.

10

On Display

On time, the carriage pulled up outside the Happy Jack. Javier Jara stepped down, removed his leather glove and shook Corbin's hand. 'Ignacio is looking forward to meeting you, Señor.'

'It's mutual, Javier.'

The hacienda was not far. The carriage turned left out of town and they rode about a mile to the east. They approached high wooden double doors set in an arch in the whitewashed boundary wall. The doors were opened by two *campesinos*. At the other side of a huge quadrangle was a single-story white adobe building, its veranda a series of elegant arches. Beyond and behind the hacienda grounds a narrow trail wound up through rocky terrain. Javier pointed. 'That leads to the mine

— but it is only suitable for horses and mules, not wagons. That is why the ore must pass through the town.'

Corbin nodded and eyed the wall parapets. About six men paced on sentry duty. He could see that they were not gunfighters but field workers. Impressive though the place was, it could not deflect for long a sustained attack with Winchesters.

A short stout man dressed in a fine light blue suit walked on to the veranda and waved at Javier. 'That is Ignacio.'

Drawing the carriage alongside the veranda, Javier applied the brake. Corbin climbed down and walked over to his host. They shook hands — Ignacio's grip was firm and strong. His eyes were almond-shaped and like bright pebbles, shaded by a prominent lined brow. 'Pleased to meet you, Señor Molina.'

'Likewise, *señor*.'

Clapping Corbin on the back, Ignacio said, 'Let us dispense with the formalities. A drink, Corbin, your ride out here

213

must have been dusty, no?'

'I always appreciate a drink, Ignacio,' Corbin replied, smiling. He was not surprised that he felt himself relax; he'd always found Latins to be gregarious and friendly, once the ice was broken, and Ignacio was no different. Within minutes, it was as if they'd known each other for years.

The lounge was huge and furnished with heavy, dark wood. Colourful hangings relieved the whiteness of the walls. A wide stone fireplace dominated one side of the room, while a long wooden table with six chairs filled the other. Easy chairs were arranged round the fireplace, which was set with huge logs. Here, they sat, nursing crystal goblets of rich ruby-red wine.

'My cousin came to convince me that I should hire gunmen to defeat the Walkers. Now he has changed his tune and says I should wait. All because of what you have said, Corbin.' He gestured with his glass. 'Why is that?'

Corbin put his glass on the stone

base of the fireplace, fished out his badge and explained his reason for being here.

'It seems a formidable task you have been set,' Ignacio remarked. He sipped his drink contemplatively.

'I've done it before.' Corbin felt like saying that it didn't get any easier, but refrained. 'Leave it to me, Ignacio. If I can't find a solution in a week, then go ahead with the hiring.'

'A week? What can you accomplish in a week?'

'I'm well into my report. It already looks damning for the Walkers. I have a few more people to see, then I intend interviewing the Walkers tomorrow morning. After that, I'll report back to Washington. I expect the reply will be backed by federal troops, who will briefly declare martial law until the Walkers and their cronies can be rounded up and charged.'

'It can be that quick?' Javier said.

'My mandate has powerful backing, Javier.'

Finishing his wine, Ignacio nodded. 'Perhaps you are right. I can wait another week.' He put his glass on a small side table and stood up. 'Now, Corbin, come with me.' He beckoned and all three walked through to the back of the building.

Ignacio opened a door to the rear veranda. Tethered to a hitching rail was a piebald, complete with ornate saddle and a Winchester in its leather boot. 'This is my gift to you, since I have learned that you do not have a horse.'

Corbin was speechless. Quite a few times he'd been offered bribes in the course of his investigations. But this didn't constitute a bribe, since Ignacio was the victim. 'Thank you, Ignacio. He's a fine animal,' he observed, walking round the horse. 'I'll return him when I leave, of course.'

'If you do, I shall feel insulted.'

'In my position, Ignacio, I cannot accept gifts, no matter how well-meaning. But I'd be honoured to use him for the next week.'

'So be it.' Ignacio eyed his cousin and smiled. Then, turning on Corbin, he demanded, 'Will you stay for lunch? Or are you forbidden to eat my food?'

Corbin laughed. 'That would be very generous of you, sir. I'd like to sample your chef's food.'

Ignacio laughed too. 'I try to hire the Swedish man from The Happy Jack, but he seems content there.'

'He's damned good,' Corbin confided.

* * *

Lloyd and Reed rode down Main Street and dismounted in front of the cantina. They barged in and demanded a bottle of tequila each. The barman asked for payment and was threatened with a pistol so he backed away. They left as abruptly as they had arrived.

Drinking from the bottle, they both strolled along the boardwalk of the Mexican quarter, knowing the men were away working at the mine.

217

Deaf to the pleas of the women and old men, they forced their way into every home and ransacked each room, breaking tables and chairs and crockery.

Lloyd laughed, enjoying his work.

Reed delivered the message time after time: 'Tell your men that they better quit town tonight or we'll torch your homes next!'

'There isn't going to be a next time for you, Reed,' said Tillman, appearing as if out of nowhere.

Reed whirled round and went for his gun. Tillman's six-gun was already out and he shot Reed in the heart.

Before Reed had collapsed to the floor, Tillman pointed his weapon at Lloyd.

Raising his hands, Lloyd croaked, 'Go easy, Sheriff. I thought you worked for Mr Walker, anyway.'

'I'm paid by the town, Lloyd. You know that.'

'Right. Yeah.'

'Interesting shoe pattern on your horse,' Tillman observed.

'Eh?'

'You were one of four murderers who shot down the Pike family,' Tillman said, his voice a deep accusing growl.

'No, it was McLaughlin and Reed, not me. He was — ' Lloyd went for his gun.

Tillman shot him in the left leg, then the right.

Falling backwards, Lloyd dropped his weapon, his face twisted in agony. 'My legs, you shot my legs!'

'That's what you did to that poor woman, isn't it?'

Tears in his eyes, Lloyd whimpered, 'Yes, I confess, we did it. But for pity's sake, let me live!'

Cocking his revolver, Tillman said, 'I can't think of a good reason why.' He glanced around. There were no witnesses and Lloyd must have realized that fact since he stretched out his hand to grab his fallen pistol.

Tillman's shot disarmed Lloyd. 'You can live — till they hang you, you bastard!'

On his way back astride the good natured piebald, Corbin mulled over his next planned action for tomorrow. He'd been into the lion's den more than once. Usually, they were overconfident and underestimated his federal powers, which suited him fine. He got more information out of them when they thought they couldn't lose or be intimidated by a lone man.

The single shot whipped off his hat and before its echo had died down Corbin had drawn his Colt and leapt from the saddle. He landed on the dirt, rolling several times before coming to rest against a hard boulder. The piebald skittered and made for a section of the trail lying in the shade of an outcrop. Annoying, that — the Winchester was still in its leather scabbard.

Two men stepped out from concealment behind the outcrop. They took turns at firing their rifles at Corbin, spitting dust at his feet. It was clear they didn't want to kill him so he holstered his gun.

When they were close enough, the gaunt one said, 'Hey, half-breed — we have some advice for you!'

Raising his arms, Corbin asked, 'What is that?'

'Get on your horse and leave town pronto!' the fat one barked, emphasizing his words with another shot.

'Mind his tootsies, Mort!' The gaunt one blasted six inches to Corbin's left boot.

'I say we finish him now, Rufe, save us all a lot of grief!'

So their first ploy was to chase him out. If that failed, then it would get more lethal. No change there, then. It confirmed his opinion of the Walkers, however.

The pair were about twenty yards away, if that. 'Mort Begley?' Corbin asked, tensing his right shoulder. The element of distraction combined with surprise, that was what he was hoping.

'Yeah?'

'Jeannie Pegram said she sends her love.'

'Jeannie, from Ma's?'

'Yes, but she hopes your brother rots in hell!'

Glancing over his shoulder at his brother Rufus, Mort laughed. 'D'you hear that? Always said she preferred me —'

Corbin moved fast. He drew his revolver and fired twice at Mort's belly while stepping to one side and using Mort's frame to shield him from Rufus.

Firing instinctively and without thinking, Rufus shot his brother in the back. 'Mort!' he wailed.

Dropping to his knees, Corbin fired between Mort's legs at the shins of Rufus.

Then he rolled clear as Mort sank forward, clutching his stomach.

Rufus had fallen on his back and was now shrieking in agony. He saw Corbin regain his feet and shakily aimed, mouth slavering, swearing.

Corbin's shot took him in the heart.

Corbin rode into town with the Begley brothers stretched over their own saddles. He tied up outside the sheriff's office just as Tillman came out.

'Well,' said Tillman, 'it saves cramming them in jail, I guess.'

'Anything happen while I've been away?'

'You expecting something to happen?'

'No. Though usually people like the Walkers start getting jittery. Start making mistakes.'

'I reckon you're probably right. Leastways, I know the Mexican quarter will sign any affidavit you put in front of them.'

'Oh?'

'I had a run-in with two Walker gunslingers — Lloyd and Reed. Lloyd's in surgery but he's willing to talk. They helped shoot up the Pike family.'

'Good work, Sheriff. That's two left, then.'

'I reckon Lloyd will tell me who the

others were soon enough.'

'Let's hope so.'

'So now what's on your agenda?'

'Tomorrow, I go visit the Walkers and discuss the errors of their ways. I have enough to bring charges and close them down. But right now, I aim to enjoy a meal in pleasant company.'

'Yeah, all this town-taming makes a fellow hungry.'

'Sorry, Sheriff, but she's prettier than you. Another time, maybe.'

'OK.' Tillman sighed and stepped down to attend to the two corpses. 'I'll make do with displaying these two desperadoes outside for an hour or so, to dissuade others of like mind.'

'Gruesome.' Corbin led his horse down the street to his hotel and a dinner appointment.

* * *

She sat opposite him and her mauve dress set off her golden brown complexion. Her sleeves were short and puffed, while the scooped neckline flirted with the swell of her breasts. Corbin thought that Dr Malinda Dix looked every inch the Southern lady with her flounced skirt trimmed with ruches. Taking his eyes off her for a moment, he cut the layers of tender deer-meat and eggplant and used the dining fork attached to his metal stump; the crushed green tomatoes and Parmesan cheese added to the taste as he chewed.

'I never realized that the hotel's food would be so good,' Malinda observed, dabbing a corner of her mouth with her linen serviette.

'Surprised me, too. The chef came from Sweden and likes to try different dishes.'

'I'd like to meet him — get some recipes, maybe.'

He nodded. 'I'll arrange it.'

She smiled. 'I feel like I'm letting Sara down — her food's good too.'

'It is. But it's nice to be adventurous occasionally.'

Her autumn-leaf eyes glinted and her

cheeks dimpled. 'That's why I'm here now, eating with you.'

'Do you cook much?'

She shook her head. 'Not as much as I'd like, but if I had a guest every now and then it would be nice to offer something different, you know?'

'Every now and then?' he queried, his voice slightly crest-fallen.

'You'd like to be my guest?'

'Or you could be mine,' he suggested, lowering his knife and eyeing the stairs that led up from the restaurant to the rooms.

Her silky smooth cheeks flushed slightly.

* * *

Mrs Walker's cheeks took on a mottled appearance as she paced up and down the library. 'I don't believe it!' She rounded on Angus McLaughlin. 'You say the Begleys were on display — dead?'

'Aye, ma'am.' He shrugged. 'Some town marshals do it — a kind of deterrent.'

226

'What about Reed and Lloyd,' she asked. 'Did they scare the Mexicans?'

Pursing his lips, McLaughlin looked away. 'No, ma'am — Tillman stopped them. Killed Reed and nigh killed Lloyd. He's been patched up but I doubt he'll walk or ride again.'

Slamming her lace-gloved fist down on her son's desk, Mrs Walker glared. 'Your sheriff's not helping matters, son, is he?'

'No, Ma.'

'I thought you paid him to get rid of Clegg?'

'Well, he did that, didn't he?'

'Maybe so, maybe not. We don't know for sure, do we?'

McLaughlin interrupted. 'Well, we know for sure who killed the Begleys, ma'am.'

'That stranger, I suppose?'

'Yes, ma'am. I was speaking to the cobbler Moyle earlier. He saw Molina bring them both in.'

'Molina? Did you say Molina?' she demanded.

'Yes, ma'am. Corbin Molina — a

marshal of some sort.'

Mrs Walker stared and slowly turned to face her son. They exchanged dark looks and then she said, her tone icy cold, 'Bring this Molina man here tonight, Angus.'

'I'm a little short-handed all of a sudden, ma'am.'

'I have an idea,' she said, smiling wickedly.

* * *

'I've come to pick up the private effects of the Begleys,' McLaughlin explained, standing in front of Tillman, who lounged at his sheriff's desk.

'All right.' Tillman rummaged in his side drawer. Out of the corner of his eye he saw the movement and shifted sideways, but not enough and the barrel of McLaughlin's revolver slammed into his temple. He fell to the floorboards, unconscious.

McLaughlin was tempted to shoot the sheriff but didn't want to attract any undue attention. A Bowie knife would have served — but, hell, he didn't have time for this.

He crossed the room, plucked the bunch of jail keys from a hook and opened the door into a short corridor.

Another door led into the jail area — six cells, three on each side. Occupying them were Quinn and Scully on one side and the two Grangers on the other.

'Angus, I knew you'd get us out!' exclaimed Scully.

'Quiet, we don't want to wake the whole town!' McLaughlin said in a hushed voice as he tried the keys on Scully's cell door.

'Hey, what about us!' Arnie shouted.

'Quiet!' McLaughlin snapped.

Scully's door swung open and McLaughlin went to Quinn's.

'Please let us out,' Stella said in a velvety tone.

Studying the state of Scully, McLaughlin realized that he needed all the help he could get. After letting out Quinn, he turned to Arnie. 'If I let you two out, will you help us?'

'What's in it for us?' Arnie asked.

Stella laughed. 'Ignore my brother, Mr McLaughlin.' She pressed her ample chest against the bars. 'As I see it, you letting us out is enough. We'll be eternally grateful.'

'OK,' said McLaughlin and found the key for Stella's cell.

'Boss, what's going on?' Quinn asked. 'Why d'you need them two?'

Giving the bunch to Stella, he said, 'Let your brother out.' He turned to Quinn and Scully. 'In case you hadn't heard, the Begleys are dead, Reed's dead and Lloyd's busted bad.'

'Jeezus!' exclaimed Quinn.

'Tonight, we've got to take Molina to the Walkers — in one piece — and we have a special task out at the hacienda as well. That's why we need these two.'

'I'll help you get Molina,' purred Stella.

11

The Oddest Proposal

'Tomorrow, honey, it will all be over,' Corbin said, cupping Malinda's melon-shaped breasts and kissing them. A light scent of lemon verbena clung to her skin.

'It's a dangerous game you play,' she whispered, running a finger over the welts in his shoulder.

'With you — or the Walkers?'

'Oh, the Walkers. This is no game we play, darling Corbin. This is serious.' She kissed him and for the second time this night they made love, though now it was languorous and not a frenzied catching up of lost years.

Malinda had amputated many limbs during the carnage of the war, and his hand had been just one more. But their strange affinity for poetry drew them together while he convalesced. She preferred Rossetti — 'because at least she rhymes most of the time!' He argued that Whitman championed the individual and the complexity of the human body and mind. They spent many an hour going over those books, swapping quotations. Then, a couple of months later, the war ended and they went their separate ways.

Of course, each day he was reminded of her. He feared he had lost her. But even if she had been found, he felt she was unattainable. Until they met again and it was as if their courtship had never stopped, that those empty years had never happened.

The fact that she was eight years older did not matter; the war had aged him beyond his physical age.

Afterwards, they talked, to catch up on the past.

Corbin had returned to his home town to find that the Buford family had sold up and left. His girl Jean had gone too. He asked around the town for any clues as to their whereabouts. Nobody could help. The most likely person who could provide any answers was the town lawyer, since he dealt with the Bufords' land and house sale, but unfortunately he died in a dark alley at the hands of a robber and ironically the lawyer's office was burnt to the ground the next night.

At least something good came of his return. The town blacksmith was a clever man and constructed the leather and metal contraption he wore, though it had been refined over the years since.

*　*　*

Malinda marvelled at his resilience. She had continued with her medical work and gained recognition, though not in the cities and their hospitals. A few towns out West viewed her with suspicion, but gradually she overcame their prejudices and became a useful member of their communities.

'Why did you keep moving?' he asked gently.

'A male doctor invariably came along

and set up his practice in competition with mine.' She shrugged. 'There are plenty of small towns who'll be glad of any doctor — even if it's a woman.'

'Indeed, and you're all woman,' he murmured, and she proved it.

Later, she whispered, 'I remember. Do you want to say it now?'

'Why not?' he whispered. His features becoming rather serious, he sat up, bedclothes rumpled around them. He took her hand in his. 'You've taken my hand. You might as well have my heart. It belongs to you, Malinda.'

Impulsively hugging him, she sobbed, 'That's the oddest proposal I've had, but the answer's 'yes'!'

* * *

The bedroom door burst open and before Corbin could reach for his holstered gun on the bedpost, McLaughlin strode in with his revolver aimed at him.

'Don't try it!'

'Well, look at the love birds!' purred

Stella, her six-gun shaking slightly.

Corbin glimpsed Arnie and Scully out in the passageway. He hung on to the hope that if they wanted him dead, they'd have come in blasting.

McLaughlin snatched Malinda's green dress off the back of a chair. 'Get dressed, the pair of you!' he ordered, flinging the garment at her.

'Spoilsport,' moaned Stella, her eyes on Corbin, her tongue licking her lips.

Hurriedly, Corbin slipped into his pants and then reached for his hook harness.

'No, Molina, you don't get to wear that!' snarled McLaughlin. 'Scully isn't anxious for you to use your hook again.'

Turning to Stella, McLaughlin said, 'Don't just stand there ogling, shove all his things into those bags — harness, belt, everything.'

★ ★ ★

With alarming speed, the two of them were bundled out of the hotel room and

down the back stairs. It was dark, but
the full moon provided sufficient illumi-
nation. Corbin noticed that Quinn was
leading his piebald behind them. They
passed two business lots; he couldn't
recall what their false-fronts advertised,
but it didn't matter. It was obvious they
were being shepherded to the Walkers'
residence.

'Stop — wait here!' barked McLaughlin.

When they had all stopped walking,
McLaughlin said, 'Grab his left arm!'

Arnie did as he was told. Stella
withdrew a Bowie knife and cut a long
slit down the inner arm, drawing
copious blood. She uttered a pleasur-
able moan as she ran her free hand over
the blood and daubed it over the neck
and saddle of Corbin's horse.

'That'll do!' McLaughlin whispered.
'Now go, the three of you!'

Corbin and Malinda were left with
McLaughlin and Stella, while Quinn,
Arnie and Scully took the piebald away.

'What do they want with my horse?'

Corbin enquired.

'Wouldn't you like to know?' whispered Stella.

'Come on, I haven't got time for this nonsense.' McLaughlin prodded his barrel against Malinda. 'Don't try anything, Molina, or the doc dies!'

★   ★   ★

Quinn let Corbin's horse go when they were near to the hacienda gates. The animal quickly caught the scent of its old home and whinnied. Within minutes, one of the gates was opened and the horse was taken inside.

Not long afterwards, there was a commotion of shouting and horses scuffling and four riders emerged from the hacienda entrance.

'Yes, he's with them,' confirmed Quinn.

They tracked the riders for about twenty minutes, till they were far enough away from the hacienda. Then they split up and bushwhacked Ignacio and his men in a gully. Three men — two of them wounded — were easily a match for four, when they shot their opponents in the back. Only Ignacio was kept alive; he tried to flee, but they shot his horse from under him. At gunpoint he was dragged off his ailing animal and given a beating by Quinn. Arnie whooped with glee. Then they tied Don Ignacio to one of the other horses and headed back towards Walkerville.

★ ★ ★

Shoved into the library, Corbin regained his footing and drew Malinda to him. She was trembling in his grasp, breathing heavily against his chest. At the other end of the room, the Walker woman had her back to them and was dressed in dark violet silk trimmed with black Alençon lace. Slowly, she turned, her eyes like blue pebbles of hate. 'My God, it *is* you!' she breathed.

Corbin hesitated, recognizing the voice from his buried past.

At that moment the other door opened and Sam Walker stepped into the room. He wore a frock-coat, snugly fitting evening trousers, an embroidered waistcoat and a white pleated shirt. He exuded wealth and power.

Their eyes locked.

Corbin stared. 'Samuel?'

'Yes, Corby. It really is me.' He glanced with curiosity at Corbin's stump at the end of his left arm then half-turned and gestured at Mrs Walker. His greyish-brown eyes turned cold: 'And my dear mother.'

'But you were Buford — you were Buford, not Walker.'

'That was my husband's name. I wasn't going to grace this town with his name!' She spat on the floor. 'Walker is my maiden name.'

* * *

Lydia glowered at the half-breed and the memories came tumbling back. She'd set her cap at Jubal Buford as he

239

was one of the wealthiest men in the county. When he lost his first wife, Eliza, and their baby in childbirth, she thought good riddance, realizing that Buford was now available. Once she'd married Jubal and given him a son, she withdrew her love and spent her time doting on Samuel. They had arguments aplenty — partly because Jubal realized he loved only his dead wife, not her — and, after years of rows, Jubal stormed out of their ranch house one fraught night. After that, whenever they argued, he left their home and slept somewhere else. Later, she found out where he went to seek solace. The Mexican girl in the town's cantina sired Corbin.

She glared at Corbin Molina now. 'How I prayed you'd died with your mother that night!'

'You — you knew my mother?'

'Ma, what's gotten into you?' Samuel sounded distressed.

She reached out a hand, squeezed her son's arm. 'Didn't you think it strange, your father insisting on housing and feeding this mestizo whelp?' Briefly, she raised her eyes to the room's ornate ceiling. 'The absolute shame of it! Your pa sired him with that Mexican whore!' She trembled. 'I rue the day I agreed to take the boy in. Only on one condition, mind — everyone must think he was a distant relative.' It also gave her more power over her husband — and his money.

Samuel turned to Corbin, his eyes staring in disbelief. 'You're my brother,' he mumbled. He raised a hand, as if to touch Corbin, then he looked at Corbin's stump and moaned, 'Oh, my God.'

'Half-brother,' Lydia corrected acidly.

'It all begins to make sense now,' mused Corbin. Malinda lightly pressed his arm, reassuring.

'The buggy's out back, ma'am,' McLaughlin said, interrupting. 'What do we do now?'

Lydia laughed, her eyes sparkling with a strange inner light. 'Take them to the mine, Angus.'

12

The Pen is Mightier

The ride in the back of the buggy was bone-shattering and threw them all over the wooden floor but at no point did Corbin have an opportunity to overcome Samuel, who was driving with his mother by his side. McLaughlin and Stella rode close, watchful.

On their right the crest of the town's Boot Hill loomed out of the darkness, several marble grave-markers shining in the moonlight against the majority of silhouettes of simple crosses. Corbin wondered how many mine workers — or enemies of the Walkers, the Bufords — had been interred here. A few moments later the cemetery was behind them — yet he wondered who would find it their final resting place after tonight.

When they arrived at the mine workings both Corbin and Malinda were bundled out of the wagon and shoved over rough ground to the mouth of the silver mine. He carried one case, while Malinda gripped his valise. He pursed his lips: the Mexican sentry lay dead.

Over to their right was a big compound, where rail lines ran from the mine. Within the compound, Corbin knew, would be several shallow-walled enclosures, filled with ore and the processing mixture, perhaps a layer two feet deep. Beyond was the corral where they kept the horses that plodded round the big tubs, moving paddles to mix the ingredients — salt, water, *magistral* and mercury. Now it was quiet, though a bitter metallic smell lingered in the air.

Moving ahead of them, Stella tripped on a rail and swore. There were two sets of rail-lines going into the mine tunnel.

Arnie ran up from the mouth of the mine. 'Hi, Sis — we did it, we got him!'

Stella gave him a peck on the cheek. 'I'm proud of you, Arnie. Well done!'

Quinn approached from the mine, carrying a lantern in his left hand.

'Right, let's go,' McLaughlin said, shoving Malinda and Corbin ahead of him. They followed Quinn back into the mine. Wall lanterns were lit on one side the full length of the entrance tunnel. Behind them, Samuel and his mother strolled over the uneven ground.

After about five minutes' walking, Malinda and Corbin stopped. The rest shuffled to a halt behind them. McLaughlin indulged them for a moment. 'Quite an endeavour, isn't it?' he said.

Corbin gave him a black look over his shoulder and McLaughlin laughed.

It was unlike any silver mine that Corbin had seen. Usually, they were narrow defiles sliced into bedrock. Here, though, a natural cavern area opened ahead of them and it was lit by a number of lanterns that cast eerie shadows over the damp mine walls.

Different strata of rock glinted — and he could spot thick slivers of silver, apparently there for the taking. In the centre of this place a huge square hole — measuring about thirty feet from side to side — had been dug out of the cavern floor. The two rail lines ran round each side of the hole and terminated at the two sides. The ends of six ladders stuck up against the hole's right-hand lip. Hanging from the cavern ceiling above the black hole was a series of four separate pulleys, with big metal buckets suspended from taut ropes that angled down to the right of the cavern, where they were secured against a large rail embedded in the cavern floor. On their left was a wide pathway that had been flattened on the cavern floor, leading away from the hole. Corbin assumed that miners below must load the buckets with ore and they were then hauled up — surprisingly by men rather than mules, judging by the lack of hoof markings.

An ore truck was parked at the end of

each rail line, on the right and left of the hole. A mound of spoil was heaped at the edge of the hole directly opposite, as if they had been too anxious to get to the ore to bother removing all the earth that had been dug out.

'Señor Ignacio!' Malinda gasped as McLaughlin shoved her into the light. To their right, on the other side of the hole, Ignacio de la Fuente was tied to an upright roof support beam. His face was badly bruised, his lips black with blood and his jacket torn at the shoulder. He eyed them, shook his head and uttered a groan of despair, as if all hope had now been extinguished.

Corbin sympathized as he was pushed in alongside Malinda.

Then they saw Scully sitting on a rock shelf to the left; he was fiddling with a reel of fuse wire. Corbin identified a pile of boxes by Scully's feet, all stamped EXPLOSIVES, and stacked against the cavern wall behind Scully. This did not bode well, he thought, and laughed at his own understatement.

Hands clasped behind his back, as if he was on a Sunday stroll, Samuel strode past them until he reached the lip of the hole, where he stood, studying its black depths. His mother approached him from behind and her hand grabbed his. As if strengthened by her touch, he raised his head and turned his gaze on Malinda and Corbin. 'Tie them up!' he ordered, pointing at two uprights on the other side of the hole, between the explosives and Ignacio.

There was little point in struggling, Corbin thought, as Quinn and Arnie grabbed Corbin's bags off him and Malinda. They were both shoved past the black hole and dusty ropes were used to secure Corbin and Malinda by waist, torso and upper arms to separate wooden uprights on Ignacio's right.

Lydia grabbed Corbin's bags, knelt down in the dust with them and started rummaging through their contents, discarding Corbin's clothes, consigning most of them into the hole.

Samuel glanced briefly at her, puzzled, then shook his head. He kept eyeing Corbin then looking away. Maybe he had a troubled conscience. Corbin doubted it, though.

As if coming to a decision, Samuel pointed to the crates of explosives. 'Scully, time to get busy. We'll finish it for the Mexicans as well!'

'Wait!' Lydia called; she looked up from the disturbed contents of the bags, casting her eyes on McLaughlin and Quinn. 'Where's Molina's report?'

'Report?' McLaughlin queried.

She let out a seething hiss. 'Idiot!' She stood and dusted her skirts. 'It isn't among his things! He must have put it somewhere for safe keeping.'

'Does it really matter, Ma?'

'Yes, it does! I want to see who has made scandalous statements against us. Besides, he might have left instructions for it to be forwarded in the event of his disappearance . . .'

'Always was the devious one, wasn't he, Ma?'

Corbin feared that Samuel's sanity was slipping away — certainly his memory was adrift. Was it guilt or an abuse of power? Or simply inherited? Because Corbin felt that Samuel's mother was not quite sane, either.

Abruptly, Stella leapt forward and pulled out her Bowie knife. She pressed Malinda's right arm against the wooden upright and held the glinting blade against the doctor's wrist. 'Let's cut her hand off, make the lovers a matching pair!'

Lydia's laugh came out like a cackle. But her lace-gloved fingers firmly stayed Stella's arm. 'Unless he tells us where the report is.'

Stella pulled a face, as if deprived of a toy.

Lydia out-stared Stella and whispered, 'In good time, girl, you can have your fun. For now, be patient.'

Stella nodded and smiled, while Malinda's face appeared as pale as death.

Sweating, the damned stump itching

like mad, Corbin said, resignedly, 'OK, I'll tell you. I put it in the hotel safe.'

'Of course!' Lydia exclaimed in triumph. Whispering to Stella, she said, 'Put the knife away for now, dear.'

Stella obeyed with a smile on her lips.

'We can break in and force them to hand it over, ma'am,' said Quinn.

Lydia turned on him, teeth gnashing. 'No, you won't, you fool. Fine, if it had been our own hotel, fine. The Presidential would have been no problem. But I think it prudent for Molina to be seen to sign himself out. *Then* he can vanish.'

'Makes sense,' McLaughlin said.

She eyed him. 'Take Molina to the hotel and get him to retrieve the report from the safe.'

'Yes, ma'am.'

'I don't trust him, Angus — I think you should have someone with you.'

'Don't bring her,' Corbin said, eyeing Stella. 'She's just itching to shoot me in the back.'

McLaughlin chuckled. 'I think I will.'

As they untied Corbin, he relaxed a little. At least his ruse had worked. He didn't want Stella staying here with Malinda. There was something in Stella's eyes — a kind of twisted jealousy. He feared that Lydia and Stella were bordering on insanity, feeding off each other. Splitting up those two women might help.

Samuel paced up and down by the lip of the mine hole. He kept looking at Corbin then his mother, wringing his hands in indecision.

Corbin ignored his half-brother and concentrated on what had to be done if he was to have any chance at all. 'I'll need my metal stump, its harness — and my gun-belt,' he said, voice firm and confident, 'if you don't want to cause any suspicion.'

'Damn the man, but he's right,' Lydia seethed. 'See to it!'

Unhurriedly, Corbin unbuttoned and slipped out of his shirt, aware that Stella was studying his torso again, her tongue wetting her lower lip. Slowly, he shucked his shoulders into the harness for his metal stump and, once all the buckles were fastened, he replaced the shirt, which he tucked in, fastening the buttons. Then he reached out for the hook on his belt.

'No hooks!' Lydia commanded.

He nodded then, with practised ease, he one-handedly buckled on his gun-belt.

'Here,' said McLaughlin, handing over the Colt.

Corbin didn't need to check. The weight indicated there were no slugs in the cylinder. He shoved it into his holster. 'My money — I'll need to pay if I'm checking out.'

Scully scowled and handed over the billfold. Corbin made a show of counting it.

'It's all there, damn you! Three hundred dollars.'

At the mention of the amount, Corbin caught Samuel's eye. Samuel looked away. He pocketed the bank-notes.

McLaughlin growled, 'Now, let's go!'

'And don't try anything stupid, Molina,' Lydia warned, 'or the doctor dies very painfully.'

'All of you are the devil's spawn!' Ignacio shouted. Quinn punched him on the chin.

★ ★ ★

'I'm sorry you have to curtail your stay, Mr Molina,' said the manager, Mr Canaan.

Corbin leaned on the hotel reception desk. 'A little unexpected business. Can't be helped.' He was aware of Stella standing by the door, doubtless her finger itching close to her revolver's trigger. His back must present her with an enticing target. McLaughlin stood on Corbin's right, pretending to read that morning's local newspaper.

'Oh, and I'll take my bags from the safe now.'

'Certainly, sir.' Canaan raised a hand for the receptionist to go into the office to fetch Corbin's bags. 'What about your luggage, sir?'

Corbin thumbed at Stella. 'My friend has helped me with that already.'

'Friend?'

Through gritted teeth, Corbin answered, 'Yes.'

'Very good, sir.'

The receptionist came out with a saddlebag and a leather briefcase. Corbin lowered his right hand on the latter. 'Thank you. I'll just sign out, if I may.'

'Sign out?'

Corbin gave Canaan a penetrating stare.

The guest was always right. Or had he cottoned on that something was amiss? Corbin hoped so. 'Yes, of course, sir.' He swirled the register round and Corbin scrawled in the line against his entry: *Get sheriff. Help us at mine.*

Unable to resist it, McLaughlin put down his paper and leaned over to study what Corbin had written. 'Why, you — !'

Abruptly, Corbin swung round, using

the pen as a stiletto, and thrust it into McLaughlin's eyeball. In the same swift motion, he let go of the pen and snatched McLaughlin's gun, cocked and fired as Stella cleared leather. His bullet slammed into her shoulder while hers shattered the glass of the picture above the reception counter. He covered the floor space of the vestibule in seconds and before Stella could recover and get off another shot, he clubbed her temple with the gun butt.

At that moment, the doors opened a little but Stella's unconscious body prevented the newcomer entering.

Corbin peered through the patterned glass and smiled. Hauling Stella to one side, he opened the door. Jeremiah Hood stood there with Jean. 'I'm sorry, Mr Molina, but I couldn't dissuade her.'

'You paid for me, so here I am,' Jean said, chin jutting out stubbornly.

Before Corbin could answer, he spotted Tillman hurrying along the boardwalk.

'Who're you shooting now?' Tillman called.

Jeremiah and Jean stood aside to let Sheriff Tillman enter. He looked grey and blood trickled from a gash on his forehead. He pointed to the body at the reception desk. 'That looks like McLaughlin.'

'It is.'

'I suppose he's dead?'

Corbin nodded.

'A pity — I wanted the bastard to myself!'

'I take it he sprung Stella Granger, her brother and the other two?'

'Yeah. I was just recovering when I heard the shots. What's going on?'

'Your town's Mr Walker is really Samuel Buford and his mother is Lydia Buford. I used to know them — before the war.'

Jean gasped but before she could interrupt Jeremiah gripped her arm tight and urged silence.

'They've got Señor Ignacio and the doctor captive in the mine,' Corbin explained. 'They plan to blow it up with them — and me — inside.'

Epilogue

El Gancho

Since he was still supposed to be a captive, Corbin walked ahead, so he was the first to see Quinn. The man was pacing in front of the mine entrance, smoking. Quinn glanced up, hesitated then waved. Tillman returned the gesture with the empty briefcase held high. The report was safely in an envelope addressed to Major Newton, in the care of the hotel manager, Mr Canaan, who would mail it later today if things didn't pan out.

Tillman was wearing McLaughlin's hat, vest and shirt. On his right strode Jean, who was dressed in Stella's clothes. Stella had still been unconscious when the clothing switch occurred in the receptionist's office. Far to their right, slinking in the shadows, Jeremiah Hood trailed them, his rifle ready.

Corbin knew that once they stepped into the lantern light of the mine, they wouldn't fool anybody. But he felt that they'd have the element of surprise.

'They're here!' Quinn shouted, running over the uneven ground to the left of the cavern.

'About time!' Lydia said, rising from a shelf of rock beside the explosives.

Arnie said, 'I'll get the horses ready.' He moved towards the entrance.

Lydia brushed her skirts and eyed Scully. 'Set the fuses — half an hour should do it.'

'Right, ma'am.' He turned and broke open a wooden crate with a couple of blows from the butt of his revolver.

Samuel paced beside his mother, his eyes troubled, glancing from time to time at Malinda. He was wringing his hands as the group entered this cavernous area. He stared, uncomprehending for a second or two.

★ ★ ★

'You're all under arrest!' Tillman barked, raising his revolver. He moved to the right, facing Lydia and Samuel. 'Raise your hands!'

Foolishly, Quinn went for his gun and Tillman shot him where he stood.

Arnie stood stock-still, his hands raised, while Scully ducked behind the pile of spoil near the explosives. Lydia and Samuel hid behind the metal truck idle on the end of its rail.

Corbin was on Tillman's right, hunched low, his Colt drawn. Jean and Jeremiah were further on the right and Corbin signed for them to move round that side of the cavern, towards Ignacio.

Lydia whispered to her son, 'Get the woman, bring her here!'

Samuel swallowed and nodded.

'Where's my sister?' Arnie demanded, shifting from foot to foot. He stood halfway between the left-hand truck and the entrance.

'She's unconscious in a cell,' Corbin said then stopped, observing Samuel darting from the cover of the truck towards the spoil.

Scully fired from his hiding place and Tillman dived behind the corpse of Quinn.

Arnie kept his hands high but hunkered down, frightened, glancing left and right over his shoulder.

Corbin holstered his Colt and ran towards Arnie. Before the last Granger brother realized it, Corbin clubbed him unconscious with his metal stump, used Arnie's body for additional purchase and placed his feet on the collapsing man's shoulders. Then Corbin leapt above the gaping black hole, his left arm outstretched.

When his hook snagged the wheel base of the suspended metal bucket, it felt as if his entire chest and shoulders were snapped in a vice. But the hook held. His momentum continued his forward movement. He could hear Tillman keeping Scully occupied and he could see Samuel darting round the back of the spoil, heading towards Malinda. He swung back slightly and kicked to move forward again, reaching up to his stump. At the end of the forward swing, he released the hook connector and tumbled down, landing hard on the side of the spoil near the hole's lip.

He raced up the earth and rubble, leapt over the top and rolled down, tumbling into the legs of Samuel near the feet of Malinda.

Unfortunately, his pistol had fallen out of its holster as he rolled down the spoil; it lay on the ground near the lip.

Unbalanced in more ways than one, Samuel regained his footing and staggered backwards towards Malinda. He whipped out a derringer from his vest pocket. But before he could aim it at Corbin, Malinda kicked him in the spine.

Samuel exclaimed and stumbled forward, let off a shot that kicked up dust from the ground.

Corbin leapt on Samuel and disarmed him. The derringer fell in the dust.

In a frenzy now, Samuel grabbed Corbin's metal stump and tugged, jerking it, and kicked out with his right foot at Corbin's kneecap.

The blow was painful and Corbin felt his arm was liable to leave its socket at any moment.

'You spoil everything!' Samuel snarled, 'Everything!' He wrapped a forearm round Corbin's throat and half-dragged him towards the edge of the hole.

'Corbin!' Malinda screamed.

★ ★ ★

Tillman reckoned Scully had used up his bullets and needed to reload. 'Come out, Scully. This pair ain't worth dying for!'

'Maybe not, Sheriff, but the silver's mighty attractive from where I'm sitting!' He laughed and held up a stick of dynamite, which was hissing. 'This is a five minute fuse, I reckon, though I ain't so exact with measuring.'

'What do you want?'

'I want you to die!' Scully bawled. Laughing, he tossed the stick towards Tillman.

Tillman rolled on to his back, aimed and fired.

He let out a thankful breath as the bullet severed the flickering fuse from the stick. Relatively harmless, the explosive dropped to the ground by Tillman's side.

'Nice shooting, Sheriff, but I've got plenty more!'

★ ★ ★

Seeing that Tillman was distracted by Scully, Lydia slunk across the gap between her hiding-place behind the truck and the spoil. She could see Samuel struggling with Molina and her son seemed to be getting the better of the half-breed, thank the Lord.

Suddenly, there was an abrupt explosion behind her. It was deafening, and the blast thrust her stumbling and sprawling towards the lip of the hole.

Rock crumbled and a cloud of dust cut visibility by half.

She started to scream as the gaping blackness filled her vision. Abruptly her descent was arrested and her shoulder felt as though it had been dislocated.

Corbin Molina held her arm with his good hand, while her son Samuel was throttling the half-breed. If Molina died, his grip would loosen — it might anyway, she realized.

Samuel didn't seem to be aware of anything. It was as if the explosion hadn't just deafened him, it had removed all sense too.

'Samuel, son, let go or I'll die! Your mother will die!'

At that moment, Jean strode next to Samuel and pointed Stella's revolver at him. 'Loosen your grip on Corbin or I'll blast you to hell!'

'Do as she says!' Lydia commanded.

Uncannily, his mother's tone and words seemed to penetrate. He stared at his hands round Corbin's throat then down at his mother dangling from

Corbin's good hand. Tears filled his eyes. He let go of Corbin and leaned down, reaching for his mother's other arm.

As soon as Lydia scrambled to safety and Corbin sat up, gasping for air, Samuel sank back on the ground, glaring at his half-brother. 'It isn't over,' he whispered, his eyes glazed with an unfamiliar haunting light. By some strange chance his hand rested on Corbin's fallen Colt. He lifted it up, swung it to aim at Corbin.

Jean fired, a gut-shot. Samuel dropped the gun and slumped at his mother's feet.

'Samuel!' Lydia bent over her son. 'You — you murdered my son!' she screamed and pulled a derringer out of the reticule that miraculously still dangled from her wrist. She fired at Jean.

But Jeremiah stepped in front of Jean, stopping the bullet.

Before she could fire again, Lydia was knocked unconscious by Corbin's metal stump. She fell across her son's bleeding belly. Corbin hastily grabbed the derringer and pocketed it.

'Ma, Ma, what should I do now?' Samuel wailed, shaking her, but she didn't respond.

'This is something you'll do alone, Sam,' said Corbin, hunkering down. 'She can't help or guide you now.'

It was as if the shock of imminent death had restored a semblance of sanity to him. Eyes oddly like old times now, Samuel said, 'Corby, I'm sorry, I didn't know we was brothers.' His voice was quite hoarse. He noticed Jean kneeling at his other side; Corbin thought that her eyes were an odd mixture of anger and regret. 'Jean, Jean, she made me sell you to Ma Begley. We argued, but I gave in, as usual. I'm sorry, really sorry.'

Tearfully, Jean nodded and bit her lip.

'Did you have a hand in the death of the town lawyer?' Corbin demanded. Coldly, he added, 'You might as well get it off your chest before you meet your Maker.'

'Yes,' Samuel croaked. 'Ma said he'd made improper advances towards her at the reading of Pa's will.'

Corbin pursed his lips then said, 'I don't know for sure, Samuel, but I reckon our pa left me part of the ranch and land, but your mother saw to it that nobody would find out. Even you.'

The light of understanding shone in Samuel's eyes. 'That's why she got me to torch the office, eh?' He let out a short sob. 'Poor Pa, his life must've been hell with her.' His hand still had some strength in it as he grabbed Corbin's shirt front. 'We had some good times as kids, didn't we, Corby?'

Corbin nodded slowly. 'Yes, we did.' He also remembered the many times his father, Jubal Buford, had used the strap on him — not because he'd done anything wrong, simply because his wife Lydia told him; whatever wrongs were committed by Sam, Corbin got the blame — and the punishment.

Samuel's grip sagged and the last of life escaped in a whisper through his lips.

Breaking his half-brother's grip, Corbin stood up. He recalled his father meting out that painful punishment and now understood why there had been tears in the old man's eyes.

Sombrely, he went over to Malinda, clicked the stump against a knife blade on his belt. It soon sliced through the ropes binding her. She fell into his arms and hugged him. She was trembling. He eased her away. 'I'll just cut Ignacio loose, honey.'

'Yes, of course.' She stood, slightly unsteady, waiting for him to return to her.

As Corbin worked on Ignacio's ropes, Tillman strolled over and said, 'Jeremiah's going to be OK.'

'Good.' He turned to Jeremiah, nodded.

Jeremiah smiled. A nod was enough acknowledgement for a brave man.

Heaving a great sigh, Jean stood up

and left Samuel's side. She went over to join Malinda who was now tending Jeremiah's wounded shoulder.

* * *

Her wrists tied, the unconscious Lydia was put gently into the back of the wagon. 'I'll stay with her,' Malinda said, raising the woman's eyelids and checking her eyes.

Jean sat beside Jeremiah; he was well enough to drive the wagon, while Tillman trailed the horses and the dead bodies. Arnie's wrists were tied to his pommel and his reins were fastened to the rear of the wagon.

Corbin mounted his horse and rode alongside the wagon; next to him rode Ignacio.

'I think things in Walkerville are going to improve, El Gancho, no?'

'You might want to change your town's name again,' Corbin suggested. 'Start with a clean slate.'

'That is a good idea, my friend. But

first we will vote in a new mayor and a new sheriff.' He nodded towards Tillman. 'He seems fit for the job, does he not? He shot Scully before he blew us all to kingdom come — it was just a little explosion, no?'

'He's good. But have you asked him?'

'Yes, *señor*. He feels a little bad about taking Mr Walker's — no, Mr Buford's — money but not obeying the man. He says he does not normally do that.'

'What didn't he do?'

'He was supposed to kill Señor Clegg, but he told me he could not do it. Such a fine shot, too, though it went slightly wrong.'

Corbin's heart lurched when he realized how close Malinda had been. She found out later that the bullet hit the top of Clegg's shoulder, chipped the bone and ricocheted into the sheriff's throat. A bone splinter damaged his eye too. It had been a lucky escape for Malinda. 'Yes, Señor, Tillman's a damn fine shot,' Corbin agreed ruefully.

He leaned down, saddle creaking,

and spoke to Malinda. 'When did you know it was Tillman who shot Clegg?'

'Not till he came round to see how Avery was. He explained. If the bullet hadn't glanced off Avery's bone, it would have been a shoulder wound, enough to incapacitate him and protect me.'

Jeremiah asked, 'What's *el gancho*, Mr Molina?'

Before Corbin could respond, Malinda, her eyes alight, smiled up at him and supplied the answer. 'It means *the hook*,' she said. 'And that's what I am — well and truly hooked.'

We do hope that you have enjoyed reading this large print book.

Did you know that all of our titles are available for purchase?

We publish a wide range of high quality large print books including:
Romances, Mysteries, Classics
General Fiction
Non Fiction and Westerns

Special interest titles available in large print are:
The Little Oxford Dictionary
Music Book, Song Book
Hymn Book, Service Book

Also available from us courtesy of Oxford University Press:
Young Readers' Dictionary
(large print edition)
Young Readers' Thesaurus
(large print edition)

For further information or a free brochure, please contact us at:
Ulverscroft Large Print Books Ltd.,
The Green, Bradgate Road, Anstey,
Leicester, LE7 7FU, England.
Tel: (00 44) **0116 236 4325**
Fax: (00 44) **0116 234 0205**